THE
Stranger
Next Door

THE
Stranger
Next
Door

Peg Kehret
and Pete the Cat

SCHOLASTIC INC.
New York Toronto London Auckland Sydney
Mexico City New Delhi Hong Kong Buenos Aires

ISBN-13: 978-0-545-11023-5
ISBN-10: 0-545-11023-8

Text copyright © 2002 Peg Kehret. All rights reserved. Published by Scholastic Inc., 557 Broadway, New York, NY 10012, by arrangement with Puffin Books, a division of Penguin Young Readers Group, a member of Penguin Group (USA) Inc. SCHOLASTIC and associated logos are trademarks and/or registered trademarks of Scholastic Inc.

12 11 10 9 8 7 6 5 4 3 2 1   8 9 10 11 12 13/0

Printed in the U.S.A.   40

First Scholastic printing, September 2008

Lexile is a registered trademark of MetaMetrics, Inc.

For Ginny, Bob, and Mr. Buddy
—P.K.

For Carl
—PETE

THE Stranger Next Door

Prologue

*A*llow me to introduce myself. I am Pete, a cat of superior intellect and handsome features. My fur is mostly white, with several attractive brown spots. My eyes are the sweet, clear blue of a robin's egg, and I wear a matching blue collar. My ears and tail are deep brown, and a dark mask surrounds my eyes.

But I am telling you only about my outside, when any fool knows it's what's inside that matters—in cats as in people. Inside, I am courageous, clever, and capable. If you ever want to describe me, remember the three C's.

You will notice I did not mention my size. Despite what the misinformed veterinarian who gives me my checkups says, I am not—repeat NOT—overweight.

Until now, I've always written my books alone. This time, I had help. I didn't ask for help; Pete, my cat, volunteered. *Demanded* is closer to the truth. Like most cats, Pete does what he wants without asking permission.

3

He simply started adding pages to the book I was working on. I had no idea Pete could type, and I certainly did not know that he was smart enough to help write a novel. The papers that came with him from the Humane Society said only: "Good with children." Not a word about any literary talent.

One afternoon when I was working on a new book, I got interrupted, and I left my office without turning off the computer as I usually do. When I returned, there was a new page in the story I had been writing. Even more astonishing, the page was signed by its author. It clearly said: "by Pete the Cat."

I read the page; then I read it again. It was good—really good! I didn't like the way he had changed the villain from an escaped convict to a rottweiler, but other than that I was truly impressed with Pete's ability. He didn't even make any typos.

I don't know why she was so surprised that I can write. We cats are known to be exceptionally intelligent creatures. How many humans do you know who can catch their dinner in the weeds behind the garage? Who else can convince a soundly sleeping person to get out of bed at three A.M. on a cold night to pour cat food into a bowl—simply by walking up and down the piano keys? This trick works every time, although I must say the humans tend to be cranky at that hour.

The night after I discovered that first page, I purposely

left my computer running when I went to bed. If Pete the Cat wants to help me write my books, who am I to discourage him? Heaven knows writing is hard enough work that I need all the help I can get.

When I first approached the computer keyboard, I had no desire for literary fame. I wanted to write because I had heard that every computer has a mouse. By the time I discovered that the computer mouse was not edible, I was interested in the story.

Two amazing things happened that night. First, I got a complete night's sleep for the first time in the seven years since I adopted Pete. Usually, Pete wakes me up at least once during the night. Either he jumps on the bedside table and tries to knock my glasses to the floor, or if I have shut him out of the bedroom so he can't do that, he sits outside the door and yowls. That night, I slept straight through with nary a whisper from Pete.

Until then, I had been bored at night. Catnip-scented balls are fun for a few minutes, but I needed intellectual stimulation. I had told her that many times as I sat outside the closed bedroom door, but she never could figure out what I was saying. Humans are not as bright as cats are.

The other astonishing thing that happened the first time I left the computer on overnight was that three pages of the new book were waiting for me the next morning. Good pages. Pages that I didn't have to write.

Excitement crept up the back of my neck as I read

them. If he does this every night, I thought, it will double my output. Some days I don't finish even one page, much less three. With Pete's help I can write my books twice as fast. Do twice as many each year.

Make twice as much money. Buy twice as much cat food.

I should point out that as you're reading this book, the words in italics, like the two sentences just before this one, are the ones Pete wrote. You probably guessed that already.

This is a novel, so all of the events and characters are fictitious, but you will notice that the cat in the story looks exactly like Pete. He is also named Pete. I tried to explain to my coauthor that characters in a novel are not supposed to be real, but, as I've already mentioned, Pete does things his own way.

Why make up a pretend cat when a fine feline, with the perfect name, appearance, and disposition, is willing to be in the story? There's an old saying that truth is stranger than fiction. In the case of the cat in this book, truth is better than fiction.

Enough of this explanation. Here is the story that Pete and I wrote together.

The byline REALLY should read: "by Pete the Cat, with a little help from Peg Kehret." I did most of the work.

1

They're coming! They're coming tomorrow!"

Alex Kendrill sighed as his little brother, Benjie, burst through the back door, yelling as loudly as he could.

Pete, Alex's big brown-and-white cat, leaped off the chair where he had been napping and ran under the table. Pete disliked sudden loud noises, which was why he usually avoided Benjie.

Alex did not look up from his homework. "You don't have to yell," he said. "I'm right here."

"They'll be here tomorrow morning!" Benjie shouted.

"Who?" Alex asked, anticipating another of Benjie's tall tales. Benjie loved to draw goofy animal pictures and then make up stories to go with them. Alex expected Benjie to say that a green-haired dog with five legs would be in their yard tomorrow, or some equally ridiculous story.

"Our new neighbors," Benjie said. "Mr. Woolsey came

to take down the FOR SALE sign, and he said people will be moving in next door on Saturday."

Alex paid attention now. "Did he tell you anything about them?" he asked.

"Nope. But I bet they'll have a six-year-old boy, just like me. They might even have twin boys—or triplets." Benjie's voice got even louder as his imagination ran wild. "Maybe our new neighbors will have quadruplet boys or—what's the word for five?"

"Quintuplets," Alex said.

"Right. I bet they'll have quintuplets—five boys exactly my age—and they'll all like to play spy and ride scooters and draw animal pictures and invent stories!"

Pete's tail swished nervously back and forth on the floor. Five more boys exactly like Benjie was a thought too terrible to contemplate. It would be even worse than getting a family dog.

Alex said, "If the new neighbors have quintuplets your age, I'm moving out. I'll go live with Grandma."

"Take me with you," said Pete.

"Good," Benjie said. "Your bedroom can be our clubhouse. We'll set up my race-car track."

Alex knew it was unlikely that the new neighbors would have five boys all the same age and personality as Benjie. "Did Mr. Woolsey tell you their name?" he asked.

"No. He told me to quit bothering him."

"That sounds like Mr. Woolsey," Alex said. "He does a good job of building houses, but he sure is crabby."

"He doesn't like kids," Benjie said.

"Or cats," said Pete.

"Maybe they'll have a boy my age," Alex said. He liked that idea: a neighbor boy to sit with on the school bus and to eat lunch with. It might not be so hard to be the new kid if another boy was new at the same time.

Benjie scowled briefly, then brightened. "One twelve-year-old boy would be okay," he said, "as long as the quintuplets are in first grade."

"Maybe they'll have a cat," said Pete.

"What are you meowing about?" Alex asked. "Is your food bowl empty?" He took the box of cat crunchies out of the cupboard and shook some into Pete's dish.

Pete waited until Benjie went back outside before he strolled across the kitchen floor, hunched over the bowl, and began to chew. It was frustrating that he could understand everything people said, but they were not capable of understanding him. On the other hand, since they nearly always misinterpreted his remarks as a request for food, their ignorance did keep his bowl full.

Instead of returning to his homework, Alex thought how nice it would be to have someone else from Valley View Estates at school. Maybe if Alex wasn't the only one, the sixth graders who had lived around here all their lives would quit picking on him.

His thoughts slid back to the ugly incident at lunch that day. School had just started on Tuesday, so this had been only the fourth day, and Alex still felt like an outsider. Determined to try to make new friends, he had carried his lunch tray to a table where two boys from his class were eating.

"Mind if I join you?" he asked.

The boys, Duke and Henry, looked at him without smiling. Duke said, "Actually, we do mind. We don't like spoiled rich kids."

Startled, Alex asked, "What makes you think I'm rich?"

"You live in one of those mansions in Valley View Estates, don't you?"

"My family moved into a new house there a couple of weeks ago," Alex said, "but I wouldn't call it a mansion, and we certainly aren't rich."

"You took away our trails," Duke said.

"What?"

"That whole area where the Valley View houses are being built is where we used to ride our dirt bikes. We had trails all over, and the first thing you people did was bulldoze them."

"That's right," Henry, said. "You wrecked our dirt-bike trails."

"It was never your property," Alex said. "That land belonged to the Fircrest Paper Corporation for thirty years. They're the ones who bulldozed it and made it into building sites and sold it. My family had no control over that."

"You bought the lot," Duke said.

"All we did was answer an ad in the newspaper about a house that was for sale. The first time we saw Valley View, the roads were paved, the lots were staked out, and three houses were already under construction. We didn't know anything about your trails."

"Sure," Duke said.

Alex turned away and carried his tray to a table on the other side of the cafeteria. He no longer had much appetite.

Spoiled rich kid—what a joke, he thought. Mom and Dad had saved for years before they bought the house in Valley View Estates.

Alex's family had lived all summer in a borrowed camping trailer parked next to where their house was being built so that the money they would have spent on rent could go toward the cost of building the house.

"I know it's crowded," Alex's dad had said, "and none of us have any privacy, but it's only for three months. We can stand it for three months in order to have a smaller mortgage with more affordable payments for the next thirty years."

They had finally moved out of the trailer and into their

new home two weeks ago. Compared to the trailer, the house was spacious and beautiful, but three bedrooms and two bathrooms was hardly a mansion.

As for being spoiled, Alex had spent most of his summer chopping and stacking firewood and taking care of Benjie while Mom and Dad were both at work. In the evenings, he and Dad painted the house and picked rocks out of their future lawn.

Alex had looked forward to the start of school, hoping to make some new friends who lived nearby. His friends from his previous school kept in touch over the summer, but it wasn't the same as when they lived in the same neighborhood.

He used to get together with Randy and John almost every day after school to shoot baskets or ride skateboards or just to hang out together. Now they had to set a date and time when their parents could drive them back and forth. The visits had become less frequent as the summer went on, and now that school had started, Alex knew he would see his old pals even less often.

So far, only four other houses in Valley View Estates were occupied; two of the families had preschool kids, and two were couples without children. Several homes were finished and for sale, but Alex rarely saw potential buyers looking at them. He certainly hoped the new neighbors would have a boy his age.

That night, Alex told his parents about the dirt-bike trails. "The kids at school resent us for living here," he said. "They think it's our fault that their trails are gone."

Mrs. Kendrill turned to Benjie. "What about you?" she asked. "Have the children in your class been nice to you?"

"At first they didn't talk to me," Benjie said, "but I showed them my picture of the flying blue elephant and told them how he pulls the moon into the sky with his trunk every night, and after that they let me play with them."

"One boy named Duke called me a spoiled rich kid," Alex said.

Mr. Kendrill choked on his coffee. "Don't we wish?" he sputtered.

"Ignore them," Mrs. Kendrill advised. "They'll get used to the fact that there are homes here now. They'll find someplace else to ride their dirt bikes."

Ignoring them was easy to say, Alex thought, and hard to do.

Pete jumped down from his perch on top of the piano. He marched to the door and glared through the glass. How dare those boys be mean to Alex, who had rescued Pete from the animal shelter when Pete was only six weeks old!

"Let Duke ride past me on his dirt bike," Pete said. "I'll shred his tires and bite him in the ankle."

"Sorry, Pete," Alex said. "You can't go outside yet unless you're on a leash. You might get lost."

"Lost!" Pete howled. "I'm descended from mighty beasts who can find their way in the jungle in pitch dark. I know every inch of this property, and I'm sick of that leash and harness! You've made me wear it all summer."

"Maybe he's hungry," Mrs. Kendrill said, and she poured crunchies into Pete's bowl.

"No wonder he's so fat," Mr. Kendrill said. "Every time he meows, somebody feeds him."

"Fat! I am not one bit fat," Pete said. Then, to prove his fitness, he sprinted across the room, leaped to the top of the computer desk, and knocked two pencils to the floor. He peered over the edge of the desk as they rolled to a stop.

"You had better exercise that cat, Alex," Mrs. Kendrill said, "or none of us will get any sleep tonight."

Alex put Pete's harness on him, then snapped on the leash, opened the door, and followed Pete outside.

Pete flopped onto the sidewalk, which was still warm from the afternoon sun. He rolled back and forth—partly because it felt good to scratch his back and partly because he hoped he could wriggle out of the harness. It was embarrassing to walk around attached to a leash, as if he had no more sense than a foolish dog.

When the harness stayed firmly strapped around Pete's shoulders and middle, he stood, then rubbed against Alex's ankles.

Alex leaned down and stroked Pete's fur. "It's a good thing I have you to talk to, Pete," he said. "None of the kids at school will have anything to do with me."

Pete headed for the vacant house next door. He loved to sniff around the outside, especially when Alex let him climb the front porch steps, leap on a window ledge, and look in.

"This is the last time we can come here for your walks," Alex said. "People are moving in tomorrow, and they won't want us prowling around their house and peeking in their windows."

Pete jumped on the porch rail.

Alex leaned against the rail beside him, watching the crescent moon appear over the maple tree. "Star light, star bright, first star I've seen tonight." He murmured the old rhyme, then wished that he would make a friend.

With his thoughts on his wish and his eyes on the sky, Alex didn't notice the three people walking past his house.

Pete saw them. His tail twitched, and his ears went flat.

"Well, look who we found."

Alex jumped at the sound of Duke's voice. Duke, Henry, and a boy about seventeen years old stood on the sidewalk. The older boy resembled Duke; Alex wondered if he was Duke's brother.

"That the kid you told me about?" the older boy asked.

"That's him," Duke said.

"What do you want?" Alex asked.

"Just want to see which mansion the rich boy lives in."

"I told you before, I'm not rich."

"Right," Duke said.

"Right," echoed Henry.

Pete's tail thrashed back and forth. Those kids had better not come any closer. If they did, they would have to deal with the fierce jungle beast.

Alex put one hand on Pete's back. He didn't want the cat to jump off the railing and run toward Duke and Duke's buddies.

"That your cat?" the older boy asked.

"Yes."

"He'd make a mighty good meal for my dog."

"My brother's dog is huge," Duke said, "and hungry."

Alex quickly looked to see if a dog was nearby.

Duke and Henry laughed.

Pete dug his claws into the railing. "Bring your dog around here," he said, "and he'll need thirty stitches in his nose."

To Alex's relief, Duke's brother turned around and walked back the way he had come. Duke and Henry followed.

Alex wiped his palms on his jeans. Why did Duke and his pals want to know where he lived? What did they plan to do? He hoped they didn't intend to come and hassle him here at home. It was bad enough to have to deal with them at school.

Alex picked Pete up. "Time to go home," he said. "It's dark."

Pete growled once, to let Alex know that he would prefer to stay outside. The darker it got, the more Pete liked it. When Alex didn't put him down, Pete put his front paws on Alex's shoulders, butted his head under Alex's chin, and allowed himself to be carried into the house. A cat works up an appetite outside, even on a leash. It was time for a little snack.

2

Clifford dumped his load of library books on the hall table. Sixth grade had a lot more homework than fifth grade.

Rocky came wagging to greet him. After petting the dog, Clifford headed for the kitchen. He hoped Tim would get home from work early, as he had the last two nights, so they could eat dinner soon. Clifford was starving, even though he'd had an apple and a bag of chips after school.

Just before he reached the kitchen, he heard Mother and Tim talking softly. Clifford stopped, knowing he shouldn't eavesdrop but too curious not to listen. Something was wrong in his family, and he didn't know what it was.

Whispered conversations, which stopped abruptly when Clifford arrived, had been going on for weeks, making Clifford more and more uneasy. Mother and Tim were hiding something from him.

What was going on that they wouldn't tell him? Were they planning to get a divorce? He had rarely heard them argue, but Clifford couldn't think what else they would be so secretive about, and Mother had seemed jittery and unhappy lately for no particular reason.

He paused just outside the kitchen.

"We'll have to tell Clifford tonight," Mother said. "We can't expect him to do this without knowing why."

"We'll tell him as soon as we reach the motel."

Motel! Clifford blinked. Had Mother and Tim planned a surprise vacation? But Mother wouldn't be unhappy about that.

"Hi," he said, stepping into the kitchen. "What's this about a motel?"

"We have something to tell you," Mother said. Her fingers fidgeted with a paper napkin, twisting it tightly. Clifford could tell from the look on her face that the news was not a surprise vacation.

"We're moving," Tim said.

"Moving!" Of all the possible scenarios Clifford had imagined, never once had the idea of moving occurred to him. "Why? Where are we going?"

"We don't know yet," Mother said.

How could they be moving and not know where?

"When?"

Tim and Mother glanced at each other. "Today," Tim said. "In half an hour."

"Today!" Clifford said. "How can we leave so soon? We haven't packed anything."

"We won't be taking any furniture or household items," his mother said. "This is a fresh start; we'll buy all new things after we get there."

Clifford's jaw dropped. His mother, queen of thrift-shop bargains and surely the most frugal person on earth, was planning to buy all new furniture? All his life she had told him to make do with what he already had rather than ask for something new.

Clifford looked at Tim. "What about the shop?"

Tim owned A-One Auto Repair. He had been a mechanic in someone else's shop when he and Clifford's mother married, but three years ago he had purchased his own place, and now he had two full-time employees, Kenny and Lance.

Sometimes on Saturdays, he let Clifford spend the day there, running errands and watching Tim work on cars. Lately he had even taught Clifford to do some minor repairs, then supervised to be sure they were done correctly.

Tim took great pride in the fact that no customer had ever returned to complain about work done at A-One.

"Kenny and Lance can run the shop," Tim said.

"But you own it!" Clifford said.

"I'll buy a different shop. Taxes are too high in Southern California anyway."

Clifford could not believe that Tim would walk away from his business, no matter how high the taxes. Tim had spent most of his adult life dreaming of being his own boss; if he had to move to a different city, why wouldn't he sell the business first so that he'd have the money necessary to start a new one?

Something is fishy, Clifford thought. It just doesn't add up. Whatever it was that Mother and Tim were keeping from him, it must be truly terrible.

"Can I take my bike?"

"You'll get a new one," Tim said. "We're going to stay at a motel for a few days. There's a suitcase on your bed; pack as many clothes as you can in that."

Clifford nodded. He picked up the kitchen phone.

"No phone calls," Tim said.

"I have to call Nathan."

"You can't," Tim responded. "We aren't telling anyone."

"Nathan's been my best friend since we were three. We were going to meet at the corner tomorrow morning and walk to school together. Thursday is his thirteenth birthday; all the guys are going out for pizza. I can't just disappear and not tell him."

"I'm afraid you'll have to."

"What's he going to think if I don't show up for his birthday?"

"Nathan's a good friend," Mother said. "He'll think that something happened to keep you from coming to his birthday party."

Nervous suspicions began to snake through Clifford's mind. His parents sounded as if they were running away, hiding from the police or something.

Clifford's mother and father had divorced when Clifford was two. A year later, Mother married Tim. Clifford's father had remarried and moved away, but Clifford didn't know where. He never sent support money, nor did he ever write to Clifford. Clifford and Tim had always gotten along well. In Clifford's heart, Tim was his dad.

Now, for the first time, Clifford wondered about Tim's past. Before Tim and Mother got married, had Tim robbed a bank or stolen money from his employer? Had he murdered someone? With the new sophisticated devices for testing DNA and matching fingerprints, people are sometimes charged with a crime that was committed years ago. Had Tim thought he had gotten away with a crime and now the police or the FBI were closing in on him?

Clifford couldn't imagine Tim committing any crime, especially murder, but why else would he sneak away without letting anyone know where he was going?

"Are you in some kind of trouble?" Clifford asked.

"No," Tim said.

That was all. Just "no." No explanation, no discussion.

Clifford opened a cupboard and began putting Rocky's canned dog food into a bag, to take along.

"Rocky won't be going with us," Mother said.

At the sound of his name, the dog's tail thumped against the table leg.

Shocked, Clifford stared at his parents. "We can't leave her behind," he said. "She's part of the family!"

"The Olsons will take her," Tim said.

"Our next-door neighbors know we're moving, and they're getting my dog, but nobody bothered to tell me about it?"

"It isn't that simple," Mother said. "The Olsons don't actually know yet. They'll be contacted as soon as we leave. I'm sure they'll take good care of Rocky; they've always liked her."

Clifford didn't doubt that the neighbors would be good to his dog, but that wasn't the point. Rocky was his dog. He knelt and put his arms around the retriever's neck and allowed her to plant slobbery dog kisses all over his face.

"If Rocky can't go, I'm not going, either," Clifford said.

"I'm afraid there's no choice, son," Tim said.

"Why?" Clifford said. His voice broke as he struggled

to hold back tears. "Give me one good reason why Rocky can't go with us."

Mother looked near tears herself. "We'll explain it all to you later," she said. "For now, you'll have to accept our word that it has to be this way."

"Believe me," Tim said, "we would take Rocky if we could."

Clifford did not believe him. What possible reason could there be to give Rocky to the Olsons, instead of taking her along to their new home? Why couldn't the Olsons keep Rocky just until Clifford's family was settled and ready for her? Then he and Mother and Tim could come and get her, or, if it was too far away, the Olsons could put her on a plane. Dogs flew all the time. It wouldn't be as good as taking Rocky with them now, but at least they'd be together in the end.

"She won't understand," Clifford said. "She'll think I've abandoned her."

"She'll adjust," Tim said. "Dogs are resilient."

"Well, I'm not," Clifford said. He stood up, facing his parents. "If you make me leave Rocky behind, I'll turn into a juvenile delinquent. I'll never do another sentence of homework. I'll refuse to take a shower after PE, and I'll talk back to the teachers."

Anger made the words spill out like unpopped popcorn from an open bag. "I'll be disruptive in class; I'll start food fights in the cafeteria; I'll carve graffiti on the top of my desk." Clifford's voice got louder. "I'll spit on the floor and write with markers in the library books. I'll get myself kicked out of school!"

His mother gasped.

Tim looked angry. "This discussion is over," he declared. "Go to your room."

Clifford stomped up the stairs, then slammed the bedroom door behind him so hard that the windows rattled.

He sat on his bed, stunned by his parents' announcement.

Ten minutes later, Mother knocked on his door.

"It's time to leave," she said.

Clifford hastily stuffed some clothes into his suitcase, put his favorite books in his backpack, then trailed her down the stairs. As he reached for the Dodgers jacket that he had worn home from school, Mother said, "You won't be able to wear that jacket. We can't take anything with a team name from this area."

Clifford looked at her in disbelief. The Dodgers jacket had been his Christmas present.

Mother seemed near tears, but she said, "I'm sorry. The jacket stays here."

Furious, Clifford dropped the jacket on the floor. He looked around for Rocky, to say good-bye, but didn't see her. He supposed she was already over at the Olsons'.

Feeling as if he had been caught up in a tornado and was being blown away to some unknown destination, he followed his mother out the front door.

Tim waited in a white car that Clifford had never seen before. A man, who was introduced as Mr. Valdez, sat behind the wheel. Tim sat beside him in the passenger's seat. Clifford and his mother got in back.

As soon as the doors closed and the seat belts were buckled, Mr. Valdez drove out of the driveway.

Clifford twisted around to look out the rear window. "Good-bye, house," he whispered. "Good-bye, Rocky." Tears trickled down his cheeks.

He heard sniffling beside him. When he looked at his mother, he saw that she was crying, too.

Clifford hunched into the corner on his side of the car. I'll run away, he thought. I'll sneak out the first chance I get and come back and live with Nathan. Nathan's family likes dogs; they'd let me keep Rocky.

No one spoke for the first half hour. Then, as they drove north on the freeway, Tim turned to Mr. Valdez and said, "Do you know yet what our new names will be?"

"The last name is Morris," Mr. Valdez replied. "Your first name will be Blake; your wife's will be Ginny."

"What are you talking about?" Clifford asked.

"He doesn't know?" said Mr. Valdez.

"Not yet," Tim said. "We didn't want to take a chance of anyone else finding out."

Tim turned around to face Clifford. "We're changing our names," he said. "From now on I'm Blake Morris and your mother is Ginny Morris." Shadows flickered across Tim's face as he spoke.

"Why do you have to change your names?"

"We'll explain everything when we get to the motel," Tim said.

Clifford's mother said, "Ginny Morris. It isn't what I would have chosen, but I guess it's all right." She leaned forward and asked Mr. Valdez, "What about Clifford's name?"

"I am not changing my name," Clifford said. "You guys can be Mr. and Mrs. Morris and I'll be your son, Clifford Lexton, just as I've always been."

"The last name has to be Morris," Mr. Valdez said.

"Why?" Clifford said. "My last name hasn't been the same as theirs ever since Mother and Tim—"

"Blake," corrected Mr. Valdez.

"—ever since Mother and Blake got married. Why does it have to be the same now?"

"Please don't argue," Mother said. "This is hard enough for all of us without arguing."

"Your name is Gerald Morris," Mr. Valdez said.

Clifford glared at the back of the man's head. Who did

he think he was, coming here and bossing them around, even picking out new names without giving them any say in the matter?

"We have to do this, honey," Mother said. "All of us. You have to use a different name, too."

"Why can't I pick a name I like?" Clifford said. "I hate the name Gerald. I won't answer if anyone calls me Gerald."

"I think you'd better explain to your son what your situation is," Mr. Valdez said to Blake. "When he realizes how much danger you're in, he'll be more cooperative."

Danger. The word seemed to hang in the air next to Clifford, even though the adults kept talking.

"I'd rather tell Clif—uh, Gerald—when we aren't in the car. I'd like to be able to look him in the eye."

Mr. Valdez shrugged. "Suit yourself," he said.

"If I can't be Clifford Lexton," Clifford said, "then I'll be Rocky."

"Oh, honey, no," Mother said. "Not the dog's name."

"Rocky," Clifford repeated. "You can name me anything you want, but I'm going by Rocky. It will be my nickname."

"He can use a nickname if he wants," Mr. Valdez said.

"But Rocky was our dog," Mother protested.

"This way we'll never forget her," Clifford said.

"Be glad the dog wasn't called Fluffy," Mr. Valdez said. Blake chuckled.

Clifford refused to laugh. How could they make jokes at a time like this?

"Do you want to know your middle name?" asked Mr. Valdez, looking at Clifford in the rearview mirror.

Clifford glared back at him.

Mr. Valdez answered his own question. "It's Michael," he said. "Gerald Michael Morris."

Clifford did not answer.

"I'll have the new documents for all of you late next week," Mr. Valdez said.

"What documents?" Clifford asked.

"New birth certificates, driver's licenses for your parents, a marriage certificate—all of the things you'll need for identification when you get to your new home."

"What about Social Security cards?" Mother asked.

"We need to get the birth certificates first. Then you'll apply for new Social Security numbers."

Clifford's parents nodded as if that were perfectly logical, but none of it made sense to Clifford.

He leaned his head against the seat and decided to save his questions until they reached their destination.

He closed his eyes, inhaled the new-car smell, and practiced saying his new name to himself: Rocky Morris.

He crossed his arms and pressed his lips together.

Rocky Morris, juvenile delinquent. Rocky Morris, trouble-maker.

If I have to change my name, he thought, I'll change my personality, too. I'll teach them to keep secrets and make me give my dog away.

I'll become Rocky Morris, bad kid.

3

"Alex! Are you awake?"

Alex forced his eyes open. Benjie stood beside the bed, with his red jacket on over his pajamas and his blue Seattle Mariners baseball cap on his head. The binoculars that he used when he pretended to be a spy dangled around his neck.

Pete, who had been curled up beside Alex, stood and stretched, watching Benjie warily. For once, Benjie wasn't shouting, but Pete didn't trust him. He waited, ready to leap down and hide under the bed if Benjie got loud.

"Hi, Petey," Benjie said.

"What time is it?" Alex reached for his small alarm clock, blinked, and looked at the dial. "It's only six-thirty," he said, "and this is Saturday. No school. Go back to bed." He replaced the clock on the table.

"Get up," Benjie said. "The new neighbors might be here any minute, and we don't want to miss seeing them."

"They're going to live next door," Alex replied. "We'll have plenty of chances to see them at a more reasonable hour."

"You'll miss all the fun if you don't get up," Benjie said.

"I doubt it," Alex muttered.

"I'm going to ride my scooter while I watch for the moving van."

"You had better get dressed before you go outside. Mom will have a fit if you go out in your pajamas." Alex rolled onto his back and closed his eyes.

Benjie left.

Pete climbed on Alex's chest, lay down with his front paws on Alex's shoulders, and butted his head under Alex's chin. He loved the way Alex's chest moved slowly up and down as he breathed; it made Pete feel like a tiny kitten, snuggled with his mother. Purring happily, he kneaded his front claws in and out, digging into Alex's pajamas.

"Ouch!" Alex said. He pushed Pete off his chest.

Pete licked his shoulder for a minute, pretending it had been his idea to get off Alex. Then he jumped to the floor and went into the kitchen for breakfast.

"Ready, Rocky?" Blake stood with the motel-room door open.

Rocky closed his suitcase, which contained some new clothes, a new radio, and his new toothbrush.

"Ready," he said.

He was getting used to being called Rocky, although inside he still felt like Clifford.

He lifted the suitcase off the bed, then rolled it to the door. He was glad to leave. Two weeks in a motel was about thirteen days too many, especially when he had spent so much of the time memorizing details of his newly created "past" so that he could answer questions if he needed to.

The only good part had been the fact that his parents allowed him to watch daytime television, which they normally forbade. Even that had turned out to be boring.

As usual, Mr. Valdez was waiting in the car. He had driven Rocky and his parents everywhere they had gone for the last two weeks: to a shopping mall to get clothes, to a grocery store to choose some snacks, and, twice, to different motels. Now he was driving them for the last time: to the Orange County airport, to catch a flight to Seattle.

Rocky had grown to like Mr. Valdez and was sorry that they wouldn't be seeing him anymore.

As they drove to the airport, Rocky said, "I wonder what school I'll go to in Seattle."

"You won't be living in the city," Mr. Valdez said. "The house is in a new development called Valley View Estates. The houses aren't fancy, but the lots are large, with many trees. It's near Hilltop, an old mining town about thirty miles southeast of Seattle. You'll attend Hilltop School."

"We've never had a brand-new house before," Rocky's mom said.

I've never had a brand-new name before, either, Rocky thought. He hoped his future classmates wouldn't pry too much into his past. He understood now why it was imperative that nobody know who his family really was or where they had come from. He still didn't like leaving his dog and his friends and his school—but he did understand why it was necessary.

Rocky had already decided to keep to himself at his new school. He didn't want to answer a bunch of questions. He didn't want to worry that he'd slip and say something that would give away his family's secret.

He didn't want to make new friends because there was always the chance that his family would have to pull up stakes again and leave suddenly. It was better not to have friends, he thought, than to walk out on them without any explanation, the way he had walked out on Nathan.

Mr. Valdez stayed with them until it was time to board the airplane.

Three hours later, Rocky followed his parents off the plane into SeaTac International Airport. As they entered the terminal, a man approached them. "Mr. Morris?" he said.

"Yes," Blake replied.

"I'm Gus Franklin. I'll be driving you to your home." The two men shook hands, then Blake said, "This is my wife, Ginny, and my son, Rocky."

Rocky shook hands, too. He wondered if his family was going to have a driver forever.

While they waited for their luggage, Mr. Franklin said, "Your furniture was delivered this morning. We'll get you a car tomorrow."

Alex poured maple syrup on his pancakes. He had just put the first forkful in his mouth when Benjie galloped through the front door, letting it bang shut behind him.

"They're millionaires!" Benjie yelled as he raced into the kitchen.

Pete ran from the kitchen to the family room, then jumped on top of the piano. From there he could still hear and see what was going on.

"Keep your voice down," Mrs. Kendrill said, "and take your shoes off. You're tracking mud across the floor."

Benjie removed his shoes. "The new neighbors are millionaires," he said.

"How do you know?" Alex said. "Have you met them?"

"No, they aren't here yet. But a big truck from a furniture store came and unloaded a whole bunch of new furniture: beds and a sofa and tables and some chairs and a television set."

"Are you certain it was new?" Mr. Kendrill said. "Maybe you saw a moving van."

"It said MASON'S FINE FURNITURE on the side," Benjie said, "and the sofa and chairs were still wrapped in plastic. So were the lamp shades."

"How nice to have new furniture in their new house," Mrs. Kendrill said as she looked at the scuffed tables and worn couch in the family room.

"If these folks were wealthy," Mr. Kendrill said, "they would more likely have bought a custom-built home, not one here in Valley View."

"Then another truck came," Benjie said, "and brought a new washer and dryer. And then—"

"I hope you stayed out of the way," Mrs. Kendrill said.

"I rode my scooter and watched. I asked the men from the furniture store who the neighbors are, but they didn't know. Neither did the men from the appliance store."

"Just because they have new furniture doesn't make them millionaires," Alex said.

"I bet they'll have a new car, too."

"You mustn't jump to conclusions," Mr. Kendrill said. "Their financial status is none of our business, anyway, so don't go asking them how much money they have."

Benjie looked offended. "I know better than to ask how much money they have," he said.

"Have some pancakes, Benjie," Mrs. Kendrill said. "I was just going to call you."

"Is it okay if I sit on the front steps while I eat?" Benjie asked. "I don't want to miss anything."

"Heaven forbid," Mr. Kendrill said.

"Maybe the quintuplets will all have fancy mountain bikes, and they'll let me ride them sometimes," Benjie said as he got a plate of pancakes. "Maybe they're so rich they'll all go to Florida for their vacation and invite me to go along."

"What quintuplets?" Mrs. Kendrill said.

"The boys who are moving in next door," Benjie said. "Five of them, all my age." Then he carried his breakfast outside and sat on the front porch to eat.

"I hope that's another of his fantasies," Mr. Kendrill said.

"It is," Alex said.

"Good. I wouldn't want to have to move when we're barely settled."

Pete looked at his calm family, quietly enjoying breakfast, and decided it was time for a cat fit. He leaped to the top of the sofa, ran from one end to the other, jumped to the floor, raced into the kitchen, then hopped on top of the refrigerator. He reached a paw over the top and pushed at the magnets that held family pictures, a grocery list, and Benjie's artwork. Two of the magnets fell to the floor; the pictures they had held fluttered after them.

Pete jumped down. He batted one of the magnets across the floor, ran after it, pounced on it, rolled around while he kicked at it with his hind feet, then batted it some more until it went under the sofa.

"My toy is gone!" Pete shrieked. "I can't reach my toy!" He jumped to the small end table beside the sofa.

"I don't know what gets into that cat," Mrs. Kendrill said. "Sometimes he goes completely loony."

"Maybe he's lonesome," Mr. Kendrill said. "Maybe we should get another cat so he has someone to play with."

Pete stopped rubbing his face against the lamp shade. "Share my food?" Pete said. "Share my litter pan? Let another cat sit on Alex's lap? No! If you bring another cat in here, the fur will fly. The new cat will never have a minute's peace, and neither will you."

"I'm not sure we need two cats," Mrs. Kendrill said. "Pete is more than I can handle."

Alex said, "I'll take Pete outside as soon as I finish eating. That will settle him down." He helped himself to another pancake. He hoped Benjie was wrong about the new neighbors being millionaires. So much new furniture did sound as if they had money to spare, and that thought made Alex uneasy.

If it weren't for Duke, Alex wouldn't care if the neighbors were wealthy or not, but he knew Duke would care. He didn't understand why Duke was so against people who had money. Was it jealousy? Why did Duke assume

Alex's family was well-off? Was it just an excuse to act mean?

Although Alex hoped for a neighbor boy his age, he didn't want the boy to be rich. He could just imagine how Duke and his buddies would react if they found out that the new boy was wealthy.

They would never quit picking on him—or me, Alex thought. Life at school would be totally miserable.

4

Time to come in, Benjie," Mrs. Kendrill called.

"But they aren't here yet."

"It's getting dark. They probably aren't coming until tomorrow."

"Mr. Woolsey said they were coming Saturday."

"Maybe he meant next week, or something might have delayed them. Put your scooter in the garage; it's supposed to rain tonight. Then come in and get undressed; your bath is ready."

Benjie trudged into the house. He took off his shoes but carried his binoculars with him into the bathroom.

Alex, who was watching a movie with Pete on his lap, felt sorry for his brother. Benjie had spent the entire day either riding his scooter past the neighbors' house or sitting on the front porch looking up the street through his binoculars, hoping to catch the first glimpse of the new family.

Half an hour later, just as Alex's movie got to the most exciting part, Benjie ran into the living room and yelled, "They're here!"

Pete, startled out of his dream of catching a mouse, dug his back claws into Alex's thighs and shoved off.

"Ouch!" Alex said. "Benjie, for crying out loud, quit scaring Pete." He hit the PAUSE button on the remote control, then rubbed his legs.

"They just pulled into their driveway," Benjie said, "and I was right."

Alex gaped at his brother. "They have quintuplets?" he asked.

"They have a new car, a big fancy one."

"Benjie," Mrs. Kendrill said, "I told you not to spy on the neighbors. If you can't mind, we'll have to take your binoculars away from you."

"I didn't spy," Benjie protested. "I saw lights through the trees, and I looked to see who it was, that's all."

"Are there any kids?" Alex asked.

"Do they have a cat?" Pete asked.

"I only saw one boy," Benjie said. "He's about your size, Alex." He slumped onto the couch and ate some of Alex's popcorn. Then he brightened. "Maybe the rest of the boys are coming tomorrow because they wouldn't all fit in one car."

"Do they have a cat?" Pete said, louder this time.

41

"Alex," Mrs. Kendrill said. "Pete is hungry."

Alex went to the kitchen to get the cat food.

Pete did not follow him. Instead, he went upstairs to Alex's bedroom and hopped on the sill of the window that faced the new neighbors' house. Benjie's bedroom faced that direction, too, but Pete was too smart to take a chance of getting trapped in Benjie's room.

He peered through the window at an unhappy-looking boy who was carrying a suitcase up the front steps. Pete saw no cat or dog or any other animal.

Alex waited until Sunday afternoon before going next door to meet the new boy. He would have preferred to go by himself, but Benjie insisted on going, too.

Alex carried a warm cinnamon-walnut coffee cake that his mother had baked as a welcome-to-the-neighborhood gift.

"Tell them to come over if they need anything," she said as she gave the coffee cake to Alex. "I'll give them a couple of days to get settled before I go over to introduce myself."

The woman answered the door. She was about the same age as Alex's mom, but there were dark circles under her eyes, as if she had not slept well or was recovering from a serious illness.

"We're your neighbors," Benjie blurted, the minute the door opened. "Mom made you a coffee cake."

"I'm Alex Kendrill," Alex said, "and this is my brother, Benjie."

The woman smiled. "I'm Ginny Morris," she said. "It's nice of you boys to come over."

"We want to meet your kids," Benjie said.

"Rocky and his dad went to the hardware store," Mrs. Morris said.

"What about the quintuplets?" Benjie said. "Where are they?"

"Quintuplets?"

"Benjie hoped you would have five boys, all his age," Alex explained.

Mrs. Morris looked both astonished and amused. "Good heavens, no," she said. "Whatever gave you that idea?"

"No quintuplets?" Benjie said.

"I'm afraid not. We have just one son, Rocky, who's twelve."

"I'm twelve and a half," Alex said. "When he gets home, tell him if he wants to come over I can show him where the school bus stops. Maybe he'd like to shoot baskets or something."

"That's kind of you," Mrs. Morris said. "Please thank your mother for the coffee cake and tell her I'll invite her over as soon as we're settled."

Half an hour later, Alex saw a car turn into the Morrises' driveway. A man and a boy, presumably Mr. Morris and Rocky, went into the house. Alex waited, expecting the doorbell to ring any minute, but it never did.

The next morning Alex went to the bus stop early, hoping for a chance to talk to Rocky for a few minutes before the bus came.

Just as the bus appeared in the distance, the Morrises' car went past with Rocky in the backseat. Alex wondered if Rocky's parents planned to drive him to school every day or if they just had to go with him this first time, to get him registered.

Class had already started when Rocky entered and handed the sixth-grade teacher, Mrs. Bolen, a piece of paper. She smiled, spoke to him quietly a moment, and then said, "Class, this is Gerald Morris. He's just moved here from . . ."

She looked expectantly at the new boy, but he did not tell her where he was from. Instead he said, "Call me Rocky."

"Where did you live before you came here?" Mrs. Bolen asked.

"Down south."

Duke snickered.

Alex looked curiously at Rocky. When you live near Seattle, the entire rest of the United States except Alaska and Hawaii is either "back east" or "down south." It was almost as if the new boy didn't want anyone to know where he was from.

Mrs. Bolen directed Rocky to sit in the third row, in the empty seat beside Alex.

Alex whispered, "Hi. I live next door to you."

Rocky nodded but said nothing.

I'll talk to him at lunch, Alex thought. I'll invite him to sit with me while we eat. Maybe he won't be so shy when he finds out that I'm new here, too.

Lunch was a disaster. Alex saw Rocky in line ahead of him and watched as Rocky selected an unoccupied table. Alex carried his tray there and sat down across from Rocky, but before he had even said hi, Duke and his sidekick, Henry, approached.

"Where do you live?" Duke asked. "We didn't see anybody move to town recently."

Rocky put a forkful of spaghetti in his mouth and began to chew.

Duke tapped Rocky's shoulder. "I'm talking to you," he said. "Which house did you move into?"

Rocky shrugged. "It's a white house," he said. "I don't remember the address."

"You moved to Valley View Estates, didn't you?" Duke said. "The same as your friend Alex here did."

"What difference does it make to you where I live?" Rocky said.

"We don't like spoiled rich kids," Duke said.

Rocky just looked at him.

"That means we don't like you, Mr. Big Bucks."

"Leave him alone," Alex said.

Duke's hand shot out and grabbed the chocolate chip cookie from Rocky's tray. Instantly, Henry reached for Alex's cookie. Alex, who was holding an open half-pint carton of milk, tipped the carton and poured milk on Henry's arm, soaking his shirtsleeve.

"Hey!" yelled Henry.

"Oh, excuse me," Alex said. "I didn't know your hand was in my food." He looked to see if the teacher who monitored the cafeteria was watching, but she was helping a girl who was on crutches.

Duke and Henry stood there, each clutching a cookie. They glared at Rocky and Alex as milk dripped from Henry's sleeve.

"You did that on purpose," Henry said.

"I'd like my cookie back, please," Rocky said.

"So would I," Alex said.

Duke snapped Rocky's cookie in half, threw both halves on the floor, and stepped on them. Henry quickly did the same with Alex's cookie.

Alex clenched his teeth as his cookie was ground into crumbs under Henry's heel. He wanted to jump up and punch Henry, but he also didn't want to get in trouble at school, so he did nothing.

Duke and Henry turned to leave. As they did, Rocky stood, picked up his plate, and dumped the spaghetti on Duke's head.

Duke spun around, grabbed strands of spaghetti from his head, and threw them at Rocky and Alex. Henry tried to snatch Alex's plate of spaghetti, but it slipped out of his hands and smashed to the floor, breaking the plate and spewing spaghetti and tomato sauce in all directions.

Pandemonium broke out. Someone yelled, "Food fight!" Two girls shrieked. The monitor rushed to that area to restore order.

In the end, all four boys were sent to see Mr. Page, the principal. The teacher accompanied them to the office, where Rocky and Alex were instructed to wait while Mr. Page spoke with Duke and Henry.

Rocky fidgeted, waiting for Duke and Henry to come out. He glanced at Alex, who appeared just as nervous as he was.

Rocky's mind skated from one possibility to the next. Would the principal call Mother and Blake? Would he be expelled from school on his first day?

He had threatened to get into trouble—but that was before he knew the reason why he had to move and change his name. Now that he understood the situation, he had no desire to be Rocky Morris, bad kid. Yet here he was, on his first day in his new school, waiting to see the principal.

He didn't regret dumping the spaghetti on Duke's head—Duke deserved it—but he wished he could have stood up to Duke without making such a scene. He did not want to call attention to himself. He had intended to be Mr. Anonymous, a kid who blended into the background and wasn't noticed.

So much for that plan, Rocky thought. It's only my first day and already the whole school knows who I am.

Duke and Henry came out of Mr. Page's office. They glared at Alex and Rocky as they passed but said nothing.

Alex and Rocky went into Mr. Page's office next. Mr. Page asked Alex what had happened. Alex didn't know what Duke and Henry claimed had happened, but the principal seemed to believe Alex's version of the events.

"Try to avoid Duke," Mr. Page advised. "He'll make life unpleasant for you."

"He already has," Alex said.

"If he goes too far," Mr. Page said, "talk to Mrs. Bolen or me about it, but don't let him goad you into a fight. Fighting won't solve the problem; it will only get you in trouble for something that isn't your fault."

Alex nodded. What a mess, he thought. He knew he would not tattle to his teacher or the principal if Duke picked on him again; that would only make Duke more determined than ever. His best hope was to stay completely away from Duke and Henry. If they approached him in the cafeteria, he would carry his tray to a different table, maybe one that was close to the teacher.

After the boys left the principal's office, Alex spent ten

minutes in the bathroom, washing spaghetti sauce out of his hair and trying to get the stains out of his shirt. When he got back to class, he saw that Duke and Henry were not there. Alex wondered if they had been sent home.

Rocky did not say anything and he didn't ride the school bus home. Since Valley View Estates was the next-to-last stop on the bus route, Alex knew that if Rocky's parents had driven him home, he would be there before Alex arrived. Alex looked hopefully toward the neighbors' house as he went up his own drive, but he saw nobody.

Despite the new boy's standoffish attitude, Alex liked it that Rocky had not let Henry and Duke get away with being bullies. Every time he remembered that plate of spaghetti on top of Duke's head, he smiled. Duke had it coming, he thought, just as Henry deserved getting milk poured on his sleeve.

Duke clearly had not expected any retaliation for crushing the cookies. Alex had never seen such a surprised look. Maybe Duke and Henry would let up on their hassling now that they knew Alex and Rocky were not wimps. He certainly hoped so.

Alex decided not to tell his parents what had happened. He would explain his messy shirt by saying, "Some kid dropped a plate of spaghetti and it went all over." That was true, even though it wasn't the whole story. Mom and Dad would be upset if they knew what had really happened, and since there wasn't anything they could do about Duke and Henry, Alex felt it best not to worry them.

Besides, he hoped more than ever that he and Rocky would become friends, and he didn't want Mom and Dad to think Rocky was a troublemaker.

Pete smelled Alex the second he walked in. "What have you been eating?" he said, and went to investigate.

Alex poured a glass of apple juice, opened a package of cookies, and turned on the computer.

Pete jumped on the desk, then sniffed Alex's shirt. Alex always smelled good to Pete, but today he smelled exceptionally wonderful. Pete licked Alex's shirt, getting a definite taste of spaghetti.

"Knock it off, Pete," Alex said, giving the cat a gentle shove.

Pete waited until Alex was drinking the juice before he shoved his face against Alex's chest and licked some more.

"You are delicious," Pete said. "You are delectable. You are what every cat dreams of—a person who tastes like spaghetti."

"Go eat your cat food," Alex said as he set Pete on the floor.

"Would you eat dry cat food if you could have spaghetti instead?"

Alex checked to see if Randy or John had sent him an

E-mail. They hadn't. He finished his snack, put on a clean shirt, and tossed the one he'd worn to school in the dirty clothes hamper.

Pete jumped into the hamper, settled happily on the soiled shirt, and kneaded his front claws in and out. He would have purred except he was too busy licking.

Usually Alex did his homework as soon as he got home from school so that he could watch TV after dinner, but that day he put if off. He went outside, hoping his new neighbor might choose to get better acquainted.

Although Alex shot baskets in the driveway for almost an hour, Rocky didn't join him.

5

Look!" Benjie yelped. "Our street sign blew over."

The Kendrills were on their way home from their weekly Thursday shopping trip. Bags of groceries, school supplies, and new shoes for both boys filled the trunk of their car.

Mrs. Kendrill stepped on the brake, then backed the car up so they could get a closer look.

A few inches of the post stuck up out of the grass. The rest of the post lay in the ditch, but the rectangular green sign that said VALLEY VIEW DRIVE was missing.

"It didn't blow over," Alex said. "Someone sawed the post in two and stole the sign."

"Who would cut off a street sign?" Mrs. Kendrill asked.

"The polka-dotted beavers from Brazil," Benjie said. "They have the sharpest teeth in the universe. They can cut through giant trees in seconds."

"It was vandals," Mr. Kendrill said. "Hoodlums who think it's funny to destroy property and cause trouble."

"I'll bet it was Rocky," Benjie said.

"Who?" said Mr. Kendrill.

"Rocky. Our new neighbor. He's bad. He's even worse than the polka-dotted beavers from Brazil."

"You barely know him," Mr. Kendrill said. "There's no reason to suspect he did this."

"I barely know him because he won't talk to me," Benjie said. "He won't talk to anyone, not even Alex, and they're in the same class."

"Is that true, Alex?" Mrs. Kendrill asked. She shifted into "drive" and continued toward their house.

"He isn't exactly friendly," Alex said. "He goes out of his way to avoid talking to anyone."

"Maybe he's shy," Mrs. Kendrill said. "He is new in town, after all, and it isn't easy to start in a new school."

Tell me about it, Alex thought. Duke and his pal, Henry, had followed him to the bus stop yesterday afternoon, whispering, "Get out of here, get out of here."

Alex, as usual, ignored them, but it wasn't much fun to always be looking over his shoulder to see what they were up to.

"That sign's cut off, too," Benjie said. He pointed at the corner where Maple Street intersected Valley View Drive.

Alex brought his thoughts back to the present. Sure

enough, where the street sign used to be, there was only a sawed-off stump. The rest of the post, minus the sign, lay in the ditch.

Instead of turning down Elm Lane, where they lived, Mrs. Kendrill drove around the rest of Valley View Estates. Two more street signs were down.

"We lived here all summer in the trailer and nobody cut off the street signs," Benjie said. "Now, just five days after Rocky comes: Timber! The signs are down."

"I'm going to report this to the police," Mr. Kendrill said.

"When they come, tell them to go next door and question Rocky," Benjie said.

"I'll do no such thing," Mr. Kendrill said, "and don't you suggest it, either. There is not one scrap of evidence that the Morris boy had anything to do with this, and the last thing we want to do is start trouble with the neighbors by accusing them of something they didn't do. Is that clear?"

"Yes," Benjie said, but Alex noticed that the minute they got home, Benjie grabbed his binoculars and headed for the front porch, where he had a good view of the Morrises' house.

Alex thought Benjie's opinion of Rocky grew out of his brother's imagination rather than fact. True, Rocky was unfriendly. Rocky's dad still drove him to and from school each day, and they never offered to give Alex a ride. Rocky only nodded politely whenever Alex said hi, and twice, when Alex had said, "Come over after school if you want to shoot baskets or go for a bike ride," Rocky had replied, "Thanks," but he didn't come. Still, unfriendliness was not the same as being a hoodlum.

A police officer arrived an hour later. Benjie followed him inside.

Pete sat on top of the piano while Mr. and Mrs. Kendrill told about the street signs.

"The signs have been up only a couple of months," Mr. Kendrill said.

The officer shook his head and sighed. "It's a problem everywhere," he said. "It costs the county thousands of dollars every year to replace road signs. We have a full-time crew that does nothing except go out and replace signs that have been stolen or cut down."

"That's terrible," Mrs. Kendrill said. "What a waste of money."

"What's really terrible is that we're the ones who have to pay for all of it because we're the taxpayers," Mr. Kendrill said.

"You got that right," the officer said. "The people who think it's funny to do this hurt themselves in the end because there's that much less money available for road repair, parks, and other services."

"If I ever see those vandals cutting down a sign," Pete said, *"they'll have scratches on both hands."*

"In most cases of vandalism to public property, the cost is spread through the entire community," the officer said. "In this case, it will be up to those of you who live here to replace the signs because the streets in this development have not yet been turned over to the county. They're still private streets, owned by the developer of the property and the individual home owners."

Alex saw the worried glance that his parents exchanged. He wondered how much new signs and posts would cost.

"I don't suppose you have any idea who might be responsible?" the officer asked.

"No," Mr. Kendrill said.

Mrs. Kendrill gave Benjie a warning look.

"It isn't uncommon to have vandalism problems in a new housing development," the officer said. "Folks who have lived in an area all their lives sometimes resent having new homes built on land that's always been vacant."

Alex thought of Duke and Henry.

"A fine way to welcome people, if you ask me," Mr. Kendrill said.

"Most likely," the officer said, "it was just kids looking for a cheap thrill."

"I'll climb the vandals' legs," said Pete. *"I'll leave teeth marks where they sit down."*

"Your cat has a lot to say," the officer remarked. "I have two cats, but they never make a peep."

"*Of course not. Chickens peep. Cats carry on intelligent conversations.*"

"Alex, feed that animal before he drives us all crazy," Mr. Kendrill said.

Alex lifted Pete down from the piano, carried him to the kitchen, and put him in front of his dish.

"You already have food," Alex said.

"*I knew that. I didn't ask for food, but since I'm here, I may as well eat.*"

"I wish I could hold out hope that we'll find the people who took the signs," the officer said, "but to be honest, there isn't much chance of that unless they return and someone catches them in the act or we find the missing signs in their possession."

"I'll watch for the vandals," Benjie said.

"You do that. If you see anyone acting suspicious, get a full description, including a license-plate number if possible."

"I'll use my spy kit," Benjie said. "I have a notebook, a pencil, my binoculars, a camera, and thirty-five cents."

"Thirty-five cents?"

"In case I need to make a phone call."

"Just don't confront anyone," the officer said. "Vandals are like any other criminals. They can be dangerous when they think they're about to be apprehended."

"I'll be careful," Benjie said. "If it turns out to be the polka-dotted beavers from Brazil, I'll call you even before I take a picture of them."

"Here's your case number," the officer said, handing Mr. Kendrill a piece of paper. "If you need to call again, refer to that."

"I certainly hope we won't have to call again."

All that evening, Alex thought about Duke and Henry. They were so angry over their former dirt-bike trails and so unwilling to see Alex's side of the situation. Were they furious enough to come to Valley View Estates and cut down the street signs?

He wondered if he should have mentioned Duke and Henry to the police officer, but just as Benjie couldn't prove that Rocky had anything to do with the signs, Alex had no evidence that his hostile classmates were involved. If he sent the cops after them and they were innocent, he could only imagine the trouble they would cause him at school from then on. It was bad enough now.

The incident made him edgy. Until then, Duke and Henry's resentment had seemed petty, something that they would get over if Alex waited it out. Alex could tolerate name-calling and teasing, if he had to, but ruined signposts were more serious. Whoever had stolen the street signs had no concern for anyone driving in the area.

Lots of vehicles came through Valley View Estates, even though the drivers didn't live there. With several new houses under construction, there were many contractor vehicles, county inspectors, phone and power company trucks, plumbers, and others who depended on street signs to find their destinations. How could delivery trucks tell where to go without the street signs?

Pete interrupted Alex's thoughts by planting himself next to the front door and yelling, "Open this door! I want to go out!"

Pete's yowling made Alex think of a joke.

"Hey, Dad," Alex said. "Did you know I've trained Pete to speak English?"

Mr. Kendrill's eyes twinkled at Alex. "Oh?" he said. "What have you taught him to say?"

"When he wants to go out, he sits by the door and says, 'Me-out. Me-out.' Listen."

"Let me loose," Pete cried. "I wasn't meant to be locked up."

"It sounds to me like plain old meow, meow," said Benjie.

"It's me-out, plain as day," said Alex. "I could probably take Pete on television and make a bundle."

Mr. Kendrill laughed. "A talking cat," he said. "What next?"

"I fail to see what's so funny," Pete said. "I've spoken

perfect English since I was six weeks old. It isn't my fault that you people can't understand it."

"Oh, all right," Alex said, getting the harness and leash. "I'll take you for a walk."

As soon as he was outside, Pete headed for the corner. He wanted to see the downed signposts for himself and sniff where the vandals had walked.

Fifteen minutes later, Alex said, "If you aren't going to do anything but stand here and smell that signpost, I'm taking you home. This is supposed to be your exercise time."

"I don't need exercise. I need to get the scent of those vandals in case they return. How else would I recognize them?"

Alex picked Pete up and carried him home. Sometimes he thought his cat really was trying to talk to him.

6

Alex tossed from side to side in his sleep. He woke and realized he was too warm; Pete was plastered against his side, and the room seemed stuffy.

Alex moved Pete over. Still half-asleep, he unlatched the window behind his bed and shoved it to the side, not realizing that the screen had moved along with the window. The cool night air felt great on his damp face. Alex turned his pillow over and lay back down, falling asleep instantly.

Pete lifted his head, sniffing the fresh air. It smelled of adventure.

He walked along the mattress edge beside Alex, then jumped to the windowsill behind the bed. His whiskers twitched with excitement. Not only was the window open, the screen was pushed to one side, too.

Pete put his head through the opening, then wedged his shoulders through. His front claws dug into the siding on the house as he balanced briefly half in and half out the window. Then he gave a mighty shove with his hind legs and leaped down to the garage roof. From there it was easy to jump into the maple tree and go down the trunk.

Pete sat on the ground below the tree for several minutes, listening carefully. He heard no dogs, no humans, no sounds at all except music coming from a radio or TV in the house next door. Pete had not been over there since the new people moved in. It was time to investigate.

As he approached the house, the music stopped, and the only lighted window went dark. Pete crept around the entire house, pausing every few feet to smell the ground in front of him. He kept his body low, moving silently.

After circling the house, he headed for the tall weeds that grew behind the Morrises' lot. Eventually those weeds would be replaced by the backyard of a home facing the street one block over.

Pete the Cat, mighty hunter, slunk silently through the weeds, stopping once to sharpen his claws on a tree trunk. His thick fur kept the dew from chilling him, and his whiskers flicked in anticipation of finding a tasty mouse.

A car door clicked shut beyond the vacant lot. Pete stopped, aware that he was no longer alone. Soon a person walked toward him. The person wore dark clothing, and Pete could not make out the face, but he saw the large shape moving closer.

Pete flattened himself in the weeds, keeping his ears down as the person approached. He hoped his white fur would not be too visible in the dim moonlight that filtered from behind the scattered clouds.

The person carried a large container in one hand.

Pete tensed, preparing to run away if the person noticed him, but that was not necessary. Although the person passed only four feet from Pete, he never looked down.

Pete could tell that it was a man. For a moment he got a whiff of the man's scent and thought he recognized it, but that smell was overpowered by what Pete realized was a container of gasoline. It was the same pungent smell as the gas can that Alex used to fill the lawn mower.

The man approached the back side of the Morrises' house, then opened the container and poured the contents along the back of the building.

Pete's eyes narrowed to slits as he crept closer. His tail whipped back and forth in the grass like a windshield wiper in a storm.

The man poured out gasoline until he ended at two large cardboard boxes that leaned against the garage.

He took something from his pocket. Pete heard a slight clicking sound, then a small flame appeared near the man's hand. The man used the flame to light a piece of paper, which he tossed toward the boxes.

The boxes instantly caught fire. With a whooshing

sound, the flames raced along the gasoline path, quickly igniting the entire back side of the house.

The man turned and ran past Pete toward the other street. This time the container was in the hand away from Pete, so the gasoline smell did not overpower the scent of the man.

Pete's eyes opened wider as the man raced past.

He recognized that smell. He knew who the man was.

Pete waited until the man had reached the pavement. He heard a car door slam and an engine start; he heard the car drive away.

Pete raced across the Morrises' yard, past their burning garage, to the maple tree next to his own garage. He climbed the tree, walked along a limb, and dropped onto the garage roof.

When he looked at Alex's window, he hesitated. It had been easier to jump from the small opening in the window to the large garage roof than it would be to leap up from the roof, aiming for that narrow opening.

Pete was not at all certain that he could jump back inside, so he did what any sensible cat would do: he sat on the garage roof and called for help.

Behind him, the flames leaped higher, and the light from the fire illuminated both yards. Wood crackled and split. Smoke blew toward Pete, making his eyes smart.

Pete howled louder. "Fire!" he screeched. "Wake up! Wake up and call the fire department!"

Alex opened his eyes, blinking sleepily. It took a moment for him to realize what had awakened him. He lay in bed, listening. Where was Pete? Alex was sure he had heard Pete yowling, but the cries sounded far away, as if Pete were shut in a closet.

Alex got out of bed and went into the hallway.

"Wake up! Bring a ladder and get me off this roof!"

Alex listened again; the yowling seemed to come from outside. Had Pete managed to sneak outdoors?

Alex went downstairs. He opened the front door, looked out, and gasped.

"Mom! Dad!" he yelled as he raced to the telephone. "The Morrises' house is on fire!"

He dialed 911.

"Our neighbors' house is on fire," he said.

"What is the address?"

For a second Alex blanked. The only address he could remember was his old one, where he had spent the first twelve years of his life. Then he saw that one of his parents had written their new address on a piece of tape and stuck it to the base of the telephone.

He gave his address and said the fire was next door. By then, both of his parents had come downstairs. Mom took the phone and talked to the dispatcher, giving explicit directions on how to get to Valley View Estates. Dad rushed outside, ran to the Morrises' house, and pounded on their front door.

"Fire!" he shouted. "Get out! Your house is on fire!"

Alex hurried through the kitchen, into the garage. He opened the overhead door and dragged a hose outside.

"Get me down! Get me down! I'm going to collapse from smoke inhalation!"

Alex looked up. He saw Pete peering over the edge of the roof.

"There you are," Alex said. "How did you get out there?"

"I jumped out the window," Pete said. *"Come and get me."*

Alex pulled the hose to an outside faucet, connected it, and turned on the water. Mrs. Kendrill ran to help. They stretched the hose as far as it would go; then Alex sprayed the water toward the house next door.

He was too far away for his water to reach the flames, so he wet the grass instead.

Sparks flew into the air. Some landed perilously close to Alex's house. Quickly he turned his hose on them. The small flames sizzled and spit as the water doused them, but others quickly surged up again in new places.

Mr. Kendrill continued to shout and pound on the neighbors' door.

Alex saw lights come on in an upstairs window. Seconds later Mr. Morris and Rocky rushed outside.

Alex heard a siren in the distance, coming closer. Hurry, he thought. This fire's burning fast.

He could tell that the siren was coming up the hill, approaching Valley View Estates. Then, instead of continuing to get louder, it began to fade in the distance.

"They missed the turn!" Mr. Morris said. "They've gone too far."

"There's no street sign," Alex said.

Mrs. Kendrill rushed inside, called 911 again, and explained what had happened. Soon Alex heard the siren returning. That time the fire truck turned at the proper corner and found the fire, but by then the flames had reached the second story of the house.

Flames shot through the roof. Windows broke, sending shattered glass to the ground. Thick, dark smoke blocked the moonlight, causing Alex to hold his arm to his face and breathe through his pajama sleeve.

When the firefighters turned their big hoses on the flames, Alex turned off his small garden hose. He joined his parents, who stood with Mr. Morris and Rocky, watching the drama.

"Where's your mom?" he asked Rocky.

"She's out of town."

It took nearly an hour for the firefighters to extinguish the fire. During that time four cars drove slowly past, one at a time, while the people inside gawked at the fire.

"Siren chasers," Mr. Kendrill muttered.

Alex noticed that each time a car passed, Rocky and his dad turned away as if they didn't want to be recognized.

The flames had gutted the garage and the back half of the house. The front, though not as badly burned, had extensive smoke and water damage.

Mrs. Kendrill made coffee and hot chocolate and invited Mr. Morris and Rocky to come inside.

"You can borrow some clothes," Mr. Kendrill said. "They might not fit perfectly, but it's better than talking to the fire department in your pajamas."

Alex led Rocky into his room, glad for a chance to get to know him. Even though the fire was unfortunate, no one had been hurt and maybe it would result in Rocky finally becoming a friend.

Alex opened the closet. "Jeans, T-shirts, and sweatshirts are on the shelves; socks and underwear are in the drawers. Pick out whatever you want."

"Thanks."

Alex got dressed, too.

Rocky chose jeans and a Seattle Mariners sweatshirt. It was Alex's favorite sweatshirt, but he didn't say so.

Everything fit except Alex's shoes; Rocky's feet were much larger.

"You can take another set of clothes, if you want," Alex

said, after Rocky was dressed. "You might need a change, and I imagine you lost all of your own stuff."

Rocky shrugged, as if he didn't care. "I didn't have much," he said. He took a T-shirt and a second pair of jeans, plus more underwear and socks. "Thanks," he said again.

"I've never known anyone who had a fire," Alex said.

"Neither have I. When I woke up, my room was already so full of smoke I could hardly find the door. It was scary."

"I'll bet."

Rocky turned to leave; Alex wanted him to stay and talk more.

"Have Duke and Henry bothered you since you dumped the spaghetti on Duke's head?" Alex asked.

"Those creeps," Rocky said. "Yesterday in the library, Duke slipped me a note that said, 'You aren't safe in Valley View.' Then before I could say anything, he left the library."

"You aren't safe in Valley View?" Alex repeated. He stared at Rocky. "Do you suppose Duke started the fire?"

7

Rocky shook his head. "If Duke planned to set a fire, he wouldn't announce it ahead of time, would he? He'd keep it a secret, for fear of getting caught."

"That's true. But if he didn't set the fire, what does his note mean? Why aren't you safe?"

"I don't think it means anything," Rocky said. "He's just trying to scare me."

"Duke's a bully," Alex said, "and Henry is a sheep, following after him."

"That's right. They don't scare me one bit."

Although Rocky claimed not to be scared, Alex noticed that his face was pale and his hands, as he tried to wedge his feet into Alex's too-small shoes, were trembling.

Well, who wouldn't be upset? Alex thought. I'd be shaking, too, if my house had just burned.

"Maybe you can wear a pair of my dad's shoes," Alex

suggested. "They might be too big, but it would be better than going barefoot."

Mr. Kendrill gladly supplied a pair of sneakers for Rocky.

When everyone was dressed, they all stood at the window, watching the firefighters roll up the hoses and prepare to leave.

"It's lucky for us that you saw the fire," Mr. Morris said. "I was sound asleep, and the smoke alarm didn't go off. If you hadn't pounded on the door, we may not have escaped in time."

"Alex is the hero," Mr. Kendrill said. "He woke us up and he called nine-one-one."

"What woke you?" Mrs. Kendrill asked Alex.

"I heard Pete yowling." Alex drew his breath in sharply. "Oh my gosh, I forgot: Pete's outside, on the garage roof."

Alex and his dad rushed to the garage and looked up.

"It's about time," Pete yelled. "I thought you were never coming to get me down."

Mr. Kendrill got out a wooden ladder and held it steady while Alex climbed up. When his waist was even with the roof, he stretched his hands toward Pete.

"Come on, Pete," Alex said. "Over here."

Pete stayed just out of Alex's reach. He didn't want to appear too anxious to be rescued. After all, he could easily have jumped back through the window or climbed down the tree trunk or leaped from the roof to the ground in a single, graceful jump, if he had wanted to.

"Here, Pete," Alex said. "I'll carry you down. Don't be scared."

"Scared!" Pete hollered. "I wasn't scared for one second. But since you're here, I suppose I may as well go down the ladder with you."

"Come on, big boy," Alex said. "Get over here so I can reach you."

Pete crept closer. When he felt Alex's hands on his back, he slid over the edge of the roof, put his front paws around Alex's neck, and hung on.

Alex backed down, holding the edge of the ladder with one hand and Pete with the other. He went through the garage and in the kitchen door before setting Pete down.

"How in the world did that cat get outside?" Mrs. Kendrill said.

"I don't know," Alex said, "but we're lucky he did. If he hadn't yowled I would still be asleep. We would never have seen the fire. Pete's a hero."

"You can say that again," Pete said.

There was a loud scream from upstairs, followed by footsteps pounding across the hall and down the steps.

"There's a fire!" Benjie yelled. "Over at the Morrises' house! A fire truck is over there and . . ."

Benjie burst into the kitchen, stopped, and looked

from his parents to Alex to the Morrises. "Why didn't anybody wake me up?"

"We were busy," Mrs. Kendrill said. "It was more important to wake the Morrises."

"I missed all the excitement," Benjie wailed. "The only reason I woke up now is because I was cold. If I hadn't opened my window earlier I'd still be asleep. You would have let me sleep straight through till morning and I wouldn't have seen the fire truck at all."

"The window!" Alex said. "I opened my window, too, and I'll bet I accidentally pushed the screen open at the same time. That happened once before, only that time it was during the day, and I realized what I had done."

He hurried up to his room to close the window.

"You'll need to be more careful," Mrs. Kendrill said. "We've had enough excitement for one night; we don't need a lost cat."

"*Why do you think I'll get lost?*" Pete said. "*I know my way around this neighborhood as if it were the inside of the barn where I was born. Lost, indeed. Give me some credit for having a brain.*"

"I wonder how long he was outside," Alex said.

"*Not nearly long enough,*" Pete said. "*I didn't even catch a mouse. I came home because of the fire.*"

"Thank goodness he knew enough to stay on the garage roof," Mr. Kendrill said.

"That's what you think," Pete said.

"You certainly have a talkative cat," Mr. Morris said. "Here, kitty. Nice, kitty."

Pete rubbed against Mr. Morris's shoe, which was really Mr. Kendrill's shoe, and allowed Mr. Morris to pet him.

"My, he's a big fat cat," Mr. Morris said.

"Solid muscle," Pete said. "Not an ounce of fat on me."

"I understand some of the diet cat foods work well," Mr. Morris said.

Pete stomped indignantly away. He looked back over his shoulder and said, "I know who set the fire, but if you're going to insult me, I'll keep what I know to myself."

"Check his food dish, Alex," said Mrs. Kendrill. "The way he's complaining, it must be empty again."

The dish was full, but Alex opened a can of tuna and scraped some of it onto a plate for Pete. He stroked the cat's fur as Pete ate.

"Pete's my best friend," he told Rocky. "He's really a smart, good cat."

"You can say that again," Pete said. "How about some more tuna?"

Two firefighters came to the door to talk to Mr. Morris. "I wish we could have put the fire out faster," one of them said. "Since we're not a city out here, we're a volunteer department. We only have two trucks, and the other one had already responded to an alarm."

Mrs. Kendrill offered them coffee. When everyone was seated, the fireman said, "An investigator will check the house tomorrow, but we suspect arson."

Mrs. Kendrill gasped.

"How can you tell?" Mr. Morris asked.

"The fire started simultaneously in more than one place. It appears that an accelerant was used across the entire back side. Do you know of anyone who would deliberately want to set fire to your house?"

"No," Mr. Morris said, but Alex was watching Rocky, and he saw a flicker of fear cross Rocky's face. He wondered if Rocky would tell the firefighter about Duke's note.

Although Rocky said nothing, he looked worried.

"The house is new," Mr. Morris said. "We moved in last weekend."

"That's rotten luck," the firefighter said. "A fire is terrible anytime, but when you've just bought a new house it's really bad."

"We don't own the house," Mr. Morris said. "We're renting."

"You should call your landlord," the chief said. "He needs to know about the fire. He'll want to notify his insurance company."

"You're welcome to use our phone," Mr. Kendrill said.

"By any chance do you have the number for Alicia

Woolsey?" Mr. Morris asked. "That's who we're renting from. Her husband built our house, and I think he built this one, also."

Mr. Kendrill found the number. Mr. Morris dialed.

"Don't let that man come here!" Pete cried. *"He's a mean, terrible person. He hates cats. He hates children. He—"*

Pete's conversation was cut short by Mrs. Kendrill, who picked up the cat and shut him in the downstairs bathroom.

"You'll regret this!" Pete howled. *"I have information that you need. I know who set the fire!"*

The humans, as usual, ignored him.

"Mr. Woolsey sounded really upset about the fire," Mr. Morris said, "especially when I told him we barely got out in time. He thought we were moving in next Saturday. He had not yet put batteries in the smoke alarms."

The firefighters left.

"I need to make another call," Mr. Morris said.

Alex heard him ask for Gus Franklin, then tell about the fire.

Alex hoped Mr. Morris would accept his parents' invitation to sleep at the Kendrill home that night. Rocky could bunk in his room. Rocky had talked to Alex more in the few minutes while he was getting dressed than he had in the entire week since he moved next door. Maybe now they would finally become friends.

However, when Mr. Morris hung up, he said, "Thanks for the offer, but a friend is coming to get us."

Alex glanced at Rocky, to see if he was disappointed, too. Rocky had his head down, staring at the floor.

Within half an hour, Mr. Franklin arrived to get Mr. Morris and Rocky.

When they had left, Alex lay in bed with Pete beside him, thinking about the fire. In particular, he wondered why Rocky had looked so scared when the fireman asked if they knew of anyone who might have deliberately set the fire.

Rocky had said he didn't think Duke was responsible. Did he suspect someone else? Did the Morris family have an enemy? Or had Rocky himself started the fire, then pretended to be asleep? Did Rocky look fearful because he was afraid of being caught?

Alex didn't want to think that. He liked the way Rocky had stood up to Duke; he wanted Rocky to be his friend. Yet he could not deny the fact that Rocky Morris had lived next door for less than a week, and in that time there were vandalized street signs and an arson fire.

Maybe Benjie was right; maybe Rocky was the trouble-maker. He certainly kept to himself and talked only when necessary. Still, that didn't mean he was a hoodlum. Maybe he was shy.

Alex didn't know what to think.

When Pete lay down on Alex's chest and started to purr, Alex let him stay. The low rumbling purr was comforting.

Alex petted the cat. "It's been quite a night, hasn't it, Pete?" he said.

"You don't know the half of it," Pete replied.

8

Rocky got in the backseat of Mr. Franklin's car.

"There's a Holiday Inn about ten minutes away," Mr. Franklin said. "You can stay there tonight."

"Do you think they've found us?" Rocky asked as they drove away from Valley View Estates.

"A fire is not the mob's usual style," Mr. Franklin said. "If they knew where you were, they would use a method that leaves you no possible escape."

"How comforting," said Blake.

"There's always a chance that this was a warning, a form of harassment," Mr. Franklin said, "but we don't think so."

Rocky chewed on the inside of his lip. He wished his mother were in the backseat with him, instead of in Washington, D.C.

"I have alerted the program," Mr. Franklin said. "I told them where you'll be staying tonight. Someone will notify Ginny."

"Can we call her?" Rocky asked. Even though he and Blake were unhurt, it seemed imperative to talk to his mother right away.

"She'll call you," Mr. Franklin said, "as soon as she can. I know she'll be upset when she learns what happened, but right now her safety, and yours, is our first concern."

Rocky folded his arms across his chest, rubbing on the sleeves of Alex's sweatshirt, trying to get warm. Why did Mother have to be in Washington, D.C., tonight? Why did she have to go there at all? Why couldn't someone else testify during the trial?

Mother and Blake had explained the whole situation, but Rocky still didn't totally understand it all. Something about their explanation bothered him, but he couldn't figure out exactly what was wrong.

He closed his eyes and thought back to that first night, more than a month ago, when they had moved so suddenly. After Mr. Valdez took them to a hotel room, the three adults had finally explained the situation to him.

"We are moving," Mother had told him, "because I'm going to be a witness for the United States government in a major drug trial. The defendant in the case has made millions of dollars selling illegal drugs, and he will do anything to prevent me from testifying against him."

Rocky was dumbfounded. How could his mother, who didn't smoke and who didn't drink—not even beer or wine—be involved with a drug dealer? It just seemed impossible.

"When she says the defendant will do anything to keep her from testifying," Mr. Valdez said, "that includes murder. He couldn't do it himself, of course, since he is in custody, awaiting trial, but he has a network of henchmen who will gladly follow orders if the price is right."

"How did this happen? When?" Rocky stammered, not knowing which of his questions to ask first. He had to move—to change his name and go into hiding—because someone wanted to murder his mother? It was unthinkable!

"This man often uses old cars to smuggle drugs into the country," Blake said. "He buys cars that have been in accidents, then has them towed to one of his contacts in Mexico, where packets of drugs, usually cocaine, are hidden in the cars. Sometimes the upholstery is split and small packages of drugs are sewn inside. Sometimes a secret compartment is drilled in the dashboard or under the floor. More than once, cocaine was inside a spare tire in the trunk, or in a fake muffler. The cars are repaired enough so that they can be driven across the border. The drivers choose busy times when the customs agents are harried, and they take along their wives and children, to give the appearance of a family on vacation."

"Once the car is in the United States," Mother continued, "it goes to one of several auto-repair shops in Southern California. Someone at the shop—usually the owner—is in on the deal. He gets a tip when such a car is brought in so that he can remove the drugs when nobody else is there. He does this as quickly as possible, then calls an anonymous contact person who comes to pick up the packages of drugs."

"So A-One Auto Repair was one of the places the drug dealer used?" Rocky asked.

"It's one that he wanted to use," Blake said. "He called and offered us a chance to cooperate with him. If we agreed, we would get ten thousand dollars each time a pickup was made."

"Only instead of saying yes," Rocky guessed, "you called the police."

"That's right," his mother said. "When he made the offer, I said I needed to think about it. Then we notified the police, and that same day someone from the FBI asked us if we would be willing to cooperate with the government in trying to catch the drug smuggler. We said yes. When the drug smuggler called back the next day, I did as the FBI instructed: I told him we wanted the money and would do what he asked."

"We knew when we agreed to do this," Blake said, "that it might mean we would have to give up our home and our business and move to a new area. We feel it's important to put a stop to one of the biggest drug-smuggling operations in the world, even if it requires some personal sacrifice."

"If the drug smuggler used A-One Auto," Rocky said to Blake, "why aren't you the one who has to testify? Why aren't the henchmen after you? It's your shop; Mother only helps part-time."

"I answered the phone when he first called," Mother said. "I'm the one who talked to him, and I'm the one who told him yes, we would do it. I was the only contact person; I made all the arrangements."

"Not that it would make any difference at this point," Mr. Valdez said. "No matter which of your parents was testifying, your whole family would still need to go into the program."

"Program?"

"I work for the United States Marshal's Office," Mr. Valdez said. "We run the Witness Security Program. It's designed especially to help people like you, people who need to assume different identities and begin new lives because they've agreed to be witnesses for the government."

Rocky stared at his mother and stepfather, and at this stranger who was so deeply involved in his family's future.

"We pretended to go along with the drug deal," Mother said. "Two weeks later, one of the cars was brought to the shop, and we found the packages of cocaine. I called the number I had been given as a contact and gave the code word. When that person came to pick up the drugs, he handed me an envelope containing ten thousand dollars in cash."

"The FBI arrested the contact person in the parking lot of A-One Auto," Mr. Valdez said. "An hour later the head of the whole operation was arrested, too. He's the one who made the phone calls. He's the one who made all the arrangements. He's the one we've been trying to put out of business."

"The man that your mother will testify against knows that he got caught because of his contact with A-One Auto," Blake said. "He knows that he'll likely spend many years in prison as a result of her testimony."

"If she could be prevented from testifying," Mr. Valdez said, "the government would have no case against him. The outcome of the trial rests on her. We could still prosecute the contact person, but not the man who actually shipped the cocaine. We've known for years that this man was head of a huge drug-smuggling operation, but this is the first time we've had the evidence we need to convict him."

"So once the trial is over and he's convicted, we can go home?" Rocky had asked.

"I wish we could," Blake said, "but after your mother

testifies against him, his mob will seek revenge. We'll never be able to go back."

"Your mother is a courageous woman," Mr. Valdez told Rocky. "It isn't easy to go on the witness stand and testify in a major trial of this kind, especially when you know the accused so well."

Riding now in Mr. Franklin's car, Rocky's eyes flew open. His thoughts returned to the present, to the night of the fire, when his mother was in Washington, D.C., preparing to testify during the trial.

Those were the words that he had not fully understood at the time. They had been bothering him subconsciously for weeks: "especially when you know the accused so well."

Mother didn't know the accused man at all—did she? He was only a voice on the telephone, someone who had made arrangements to have a car delivered to the shop, someone who gave her a phone number and a code word to use after the drugs were found.

"Blake?" Rocky said.

Blake turned in his seat, to look at Rocky.

"I just remembered something. That first night, when you told me about the drug smuggling and why we have to hide, and about the man that Mother's going to testify against, Mr. Valdez said that it would be hard for her to testify against somebody she knows. What did he mean?"

Even in the dark car, Rocky could tell from Blake's expression that the question was important.

"Your mother and I were hoping you wouldn't ask that," Blake said, "but since you have, you deserve an honest answer. The reason the drug smuggler called A-One Auto—the reason your mother was offered the chance to get ten thousand dollars per deal—is that the drug smuggler, the man she's testifying against, is your father."

Rocky could not answer. He felt as if he were living a bad dream, hearing words that could not possibly have been spoken.

"We think he called A-One Auto as a way to help you," Blake said. "He never sent any support money because he didn't want anyone, even you and your mother, to know where he was. If we had gone along with the scheme, we still wouldn't have known his location. We believe he felt guilty about neglecting you, and he was trying to get some large sums of money to you through the shop. He knew that if your mother and I were involved in the illegal drug deals, his connection would be kept secret. He gambled that your mother would cooperate in order to make your future financially secure."

"That's why she is the only witness who can convict him," Mr. Franklin said. "She recognized his voice. She can swear that he made those phone calls."

"How did the police know where to find him?" Rocky asked. "Were the phone calls traced?"

"The FBI has had him under surveillance for years," Mr. Franklin said. "All we needed was proof that he's sending drugs into this country."

His father. Rocky had wondered dozens of times what his father was like, but his mother had given only vague answers.

"Is that why she divorced him?" Rocky asked.

"She suspected he was connected with illegal activities, but she didn't know what they were. She divorced him because he lied to her."

"Oh."

"I'm sorry she isn't here to tell you this," Blake said. "We probably should have told you from the start, but we worried how you would feel if you knew. Your mother has always wanted you to think that your father is a good person who loves you but doesn't know how to show it."

"Instead, my father is an international drug dealer," Rocky said.

"In spite of what he did, I think he loves you," Blake said. Then he added softly, "And so do I."

Rocky nodded. He didn't remember his father at all. Blake was the one who had fixed broken toys and played catch and gone to conferences with Rocky's teachers. Blake was the one who coached Little League and read bedtime stories and made him (at age five) take a piece of bubble gum back to the store when he had stuck it in his pocket without paying. Blake was his real father.

Still, it hurt to know that the man who was his biological parent was a criminal. In the last couple of days, he had begun to feel that his life was returning to normal, and now this happened.

All the anger and fear that he had felt the night when they first moved returned. He had done nothing wrong; why should he have to change his name and leave his friends and his dog? Why should he have to be afraid that someone, whose name he didn't even know, was hunting for his family, wanting to kill them?

"Doesn't it seem odd," Blake said, "that only five days after we move in, our house goes up in flames?"

"It is very strange," Mr. Franklin said, "especially on the eve of your wife's testimony. The arson squad will look at the evidence carefully, and so will the FBI."

"What do we do now?" Blake asked. "We can't live in motels forever, and we don't want to leave this area unless we have to. Rocky just got started in school; it wouldn't be fair to yank him out and start over again somewhere else."

"I don't think this fire is related to your situation," Mr. Franklin said, "so you can stay here for now. I'll talk to Thurgood or Alicia Woolsey tomorrow. They have several unsold houses that are ready for occupancy; I'm confident that you can rent one of those. You should be able to move in within a day or two, as soon as we can buy some furniture and get the utilities turned on."

At least I won't have to go to another new school, Rocky thought. Even so, he knew it would be a long time before the memory of waking up to smoke, flame, and instant fear would fade.

Half an hour later, Rocky sat shivering on the motel bed as Blake and Mr. Franklin watched a newscast about the fire. Although he wasn't cold, he couldn't stop shaking. He kicked off Mr. Kendrill's too-big shoes and got under the covers.

He longed for the real Rocky, the one with four legs and a wagging tail. He wished his dog would jump on the bed beside him right now, and lick his hand, and beg to be petted. He knew it couldn't happen.

"A dog is too easily tracked," Mr. Valdez had explained. "Airline or hotel employees see hundreds of people each week but only a few animals. If questioned, those employees could remember a dog and provide information about you or your destination."

Rocky knew Mr. Valdez was right, but he still wished he could have kept his dog. In his imagination, he could feel once more the coarse fur and the velvety ears and the cold nose.

Rocky closed his eyes, fighting back tears. He wanted

to be Clifford again; he wanted to quit pretending and quit being scared that someone would recognize him. He wanted his mother to be home, reading or listening to music or making popcorn, instead of on the other side of the continent getting ready to testify that her former husband, Rocky's father, was a drug smuggler.

Rocky wanted to go back to his old life, when he wasn't so afraid.

9

Alex hurried into his classroom the next morning, hoping to see Rocky, but Rocky wasn't in school.

Duke stopped beside Alex's desk, just before the bell rang. "My brother and I drove through Valley View last night. We saw the fire."

Saw it or set it? Alex thought, but he said nothing.

"Bad things happen when you go where you aren't wanted," Duke said.

Henry came to stand beside Duke. "That's right," he said. "Bad things happen."

"Bad things happen to people who break the law, too," Alex said.

"What's that supposed to mean?" Duke said. "Are you accusing me of something?"

"No. I'm only saying that the arsonist will get caught, and so will the vandals who cut down all our street signs.

The fire trucks got lost trying to reach the fire because the street signs were missing."

Alex watched Duke's face for signs of surprise or concern, but Duke was expressionless. Alex wondered again if Duke and Henry were responsible for cutting down the signs and setting the fire. He had heard that arsonists sometimes stay to watch the fires that they set. Is that why Duke and his brother had driven past? If so, he hoped they were plenty worried about getting caught.

"Where's your pal, Rocky?" Duke asked.

"I don't know. It was his house that burned."

"It was?" Duke looked surprised. "I thought it was yours."

Alex realized that the night Duke, Henry, and Duke's brother had walked past, Alex and Pete had been on the Morrises' front porch. Duke had probably assumed Alex lived there. If Duke had intended to set fire to Alex's house, he would have been at the wrong place.

Other kids reacted immediately to the news that a classmate's house had burned.

"How bad was the fire?" someone asked. "Did Rocky lose everything?"

"I gave him some clothes," Alex said, "but my shoes didn't fit him. Maybe he's buying shoes this morning."

By the time the bell rang, the class had agreed to bring household goods and clothing to school on Monday, to help Rocky's family.

As Alex listened to the concern of the other kids, he felt better. They apparently had no resentment toward Rocky because he lived in Valley View Estates. Perhaps Duke and Henry were the only ones who felt that way.

Alex made up his mind to try harder to make new friends. At morning recess, when some of the boys started a game of kickball, he joined in. At lunch, he headed toward where two of those boys were sitting, but before he got there Duke blocked his way.

"Trouble always comes in threes," Duke said.

Alex had heard his grandmother say the same thing. "What are you getting at?" he asked.

"Just warning you," Duke said.

"You seem to know an awful lot about what goes on in my neighborhood," Alex said.

"I make it my business to know what's happening."

"Right." Alex walked away from Duke. His stomach churning, he abandoned his intent to sit with some of the other boys. If Duke picked another fight, Alex preferred to be by himself. He chose an empty table near the food line. Duke did not follow him.

Alex wondered again if he should tell an adult about Duke's comments. If Duke was responsible for the vandalism and the fire, it was important for Alex to report that. But what if he told his parents or his teacher, and they questioned Duke, and then it turned out that Duke had nothing to do with either problem?

Duke's probably just a big blowhard, trying to make me nervous, Alex thought. Unfortunately, he was succeeding.

Duke's remark about trouble coming in threes worried Alex. First the street signs, then the fire. What was next?

I shouldn't let him get to me this way, Alex told himself. That's just an old superstition, and I should ignore it. Instead, he spent most of the afternoon wondering what the third trouble would be.

Rocky and Blake spent the day after the fire shopping for clothes.

As he looked at a rack of jackets, Rocky remembered last year when he had asked for a new jacket before school started.

His mother had said, "There's nothing wrong with your old one. You can wear it a few more months, until the sleeves get too short."

Now, as he chose a new jacket for the second time in three weeks, he wished he didn't have to do it. New clothes weren't fun when the reason for buying them was arson.

Even though the witness program was paying for their purchases, Blake insisted they shop carefully and spend as little as possible. "It's our money in the end," he said. "Ours and the other taxpayers."

They didn't have to shop for furniture; Mr. Franklin said he would order duplicates of what they had gotten a week ago, all of which was either burned up or too badly damaged from smoke and water to be usable.

When Rocky and Blake returned to the motel with their purchases, there was a message to call Mr. Franklin.

"Good news," Blake said after he hung up. "Your mother testified this morning, and everything went as hoped. She was on the witness stand for nearly an hour; the attorneys said there's no doubt that she won the case for them."

"Can she come home now?" Rocky asked.

"She needs to stay until the jurors begin deliberating, in case she gets recalled."

"When will that be?"

"Possibly as early as Monday; sometime next week, for sure."

Rocky nodded. He knew that his mother could not have prevented the fire nor could she do anything other than what Blake was doing to make this time easier. Still, he would be glad when she came home and the three of them were together again, like an ordinary family.

"Mr. Franklin also said he spoke with Mrs. Woolsey and arranged for us to move into a different house in Valley View Estates. It's two streets over from the one we had before. You'll stay in the same school and same class; we can even keep our new phone number."

"When can we move in?"

"Mrs. Woolsey will meet us there tonight at eight to give us the keys. Mr. Franklin scheduled the appointment for after dinner because he wasn't sure when we would get his message."

"Are we going to stay there tonight?"

"If we sleep there tonight we'll have to sleep on the floor. Mr. Franklin already had the power and water turned on, but the furniture won't be delivered until Monday."

"I vote for a bed and TV set," Rocky said. "What would we do in an empty house?"

"I agree."

Rocky cut the tags off his new clothes, then put Mr. Kendrill's shoes and the extra clothes from Alex in a bag, to be returned. He would add the rest of Alex's clothes as soon as they were washed.

He was glad the new house was two blocks from Alex. It would be easier not to get involved with Alex and his goofy little brother when they weren't right next door. He would still see Alex in school, but he wouldn't have to worry that every time he walked outdoors, someone would be waiting to invite him over.

Rocky knew he had hurt Benjie's feelings by refusing

to look at the little boy's paintings, and he knew Alex was disappointed that Rocky didn't go over to shoot baskets when Alex invited him. Alex had made it clear that he would like to be Rocky's friend, and under other circumstances, Rocky would gladly have accepted Alex's invitations.

I don't want friends anymore, Rocky thought. He missed Nathan a lot, but it was too hard to worry all the time that he would slip up and say something about his past, something that would give away the secret and put his family in danger. Better to keep to himself, and not take any chances.

Rocky opened the new book he'd just bought but couldn't concentrate on the story. Mr. Franklin had said that the fire could have been set by someone in the mob as a form of harassment. If that was so, the fire was only the beginning. Like a cat with a cornered mouse, the mob would keep Rocky's family constantly afraid of what might happen next.

"Blake," Rocky said, "do you think the mob started the fire? Do you think they know where we are?"

"I can't be positive," Blake said, "but I don't think so. Mr. Franklin feels it's safe for us to stay in Valley View. He's experienced in situations like ours, and he wouldn't take a chance if he felt we were in danger here."

Rocky wanted to believe that this was true, but he

couldn't help feeling scared. He wondered what his mother was doing at that moment. He wondered if the fire investigators would find any clues to the arsonist. He wondered if he would ever feel like a normal kid again.

10

When Alex got home after school, a fire department car was parked in the Morrises' driveway. Two men stood in the midst of the rubble.

Benjie, with his binoculars around his neck and wearing his backpack full of spy supplies, watched them from the family room while he ate a slice of cold pizza. "They're fire investigators," he told Alex. "They were here when I got home. They told me they've been working all day."

"Have the Morrises been back?" Alex asked.

"Nope. Not since I got home."

"My class is collecting clothes and blankets and household things for the Morrises."

"That's a good idea," Mrs. Kendrill said. "I got them some laundry soap and canned goods today, but I haven't seen them."

"The investigators are sifting the rubble through a

screen," Benjie reported. "I asked one of them about it, and he told me it's amazing how much stuff they find that way. He said people think a fire destroys all the evidence, but it doesn't."

"If they want evidence," Pete said, "tell them to look for footprints in the weeds behind the house. Tell them the arsonist parked one street over and came in the back way, carrying a can of gasoline."

"Does Pete need to be fed?" Mrs. Kendrill asked.

Alex checked the cat dish, which was half-full. "No. I think he wants to go out."

"Yes. Yes. Let me out." Pete stood on his hind legs and stretched his front paws toward the doorknob.

"I think he's ready to be off the leash," Alex said. "He's so unhappy indoors. I try to walk him every day, but it's only for a short time. He always growls when it's time to come in."

"Perhaps you're right," Mrs. Kendrill said. "Surely he knows by now that this is our house."

"I knew that before we moved in," Pete said. "What do you think I am, a newborn kitten? Humans are the only creatures who need maps. We cats find our way without help, and we hardly ever get lost."

"That constant yowling is getting on my nerves," Mrs. Kendrill said. "Let him out."

Alex opened the door. "There you go," he said. "Come home when I call you."

Pete did not bother to answer such a ridiculous statement. Alex ought to know by now that Pete would come home when he felt like coming home. If he didn't want to come, Alex could call until his voice was hoarse, and Pete wouldn't move an inch.

Pete strolled away from the house, heading toward the weeds behind the Morrises' house. He had watched the investigators from the window all day, and nobody had looked for clues there.

He had no trouble picking up the arsonist's trail. Not only were the weeds broken where the man had stepped on them, there were strong smells where gasoline had dripped to the ground.

Pete's ears flattened as he slunk along, remembering what he had witnessed the night before. He wished now that he had run after the man, but at the time he had been so shocked all he could think of was getting safely home.

Pete passed the stake with a wide pink plastic ribbon fluttering from it that marked the back of the Morrises' lot. He continued through the weeds until he reached Alder Court, the street that was one block over from Elm Lane, where he lived. He knew this was the way the arsonist had come.

Pete looked in both directions. Three houses at the end of the street sprouted FOR SALE signs in their yards; the rest of the property was vacant. An empty food wrapper clung to the weeds along the edge of the street.

Pete started toward the wrapper but stopped before he reached it. His tail swished with excitement. There, lying next to the curb, was the empty gas can. The arsonist, in his rush to get away, must have dropped it when he got in the car.

Pete stepped slowly around the can, smelling the gasoline. Then he turned and trotted back through the weeds to where the investigators were poking through the charred pieces of the Morrises' house.

Yellow tape that said FIRE SCENE KEEP OUT in black letters surrounded the house. Pete went under the tape and approached the men.

"Come this way," Pete said. "I found the gas can that the man used to start the fire."

One of the investigators looked up. "Hello, cat," he said. "I hope you didn't live here."

"Follow me," Pete said. "I have something to show you."

"Are you hungry, fellow?" the man said.

Pete wondered why humans always thought he was asking for food. Didn't they know that cats talk about many subjects, including the best places to hunt for mice, how to bat your toys under the furniture, and the delight of shredding a full roll of toilet tissue? Why, Pete could hold his own in any conversation.

"Follow me," Pete repeated.

The man put down the tools he held and walked away

from the fire site. For a moment Pete thought the man was actually going to follow him. Instead the man went to his car, which was parked in the Morrises' driveway, and got in. Leaving the door open, he unwrapped a sandwich, broke off a piece of ham, and tossed it toward Pete.

After swallowing the ham, Pete said, "Thanks, but I didn't come to eat lunch with you. I came to show you some evidence." He walked a few steps toward the back of the lot.

The man stayed in his car, eating the sandwich.

Pete ran to the yellow tape, grabbed it in his teeth, and took off across the backyard. A length of tape snapped off.

"Hey!" The man laid his sandwich on the car seat, then ran after Pete. "Come back here with that."

Pete raced through the weeds with ten feet of tape trailing after him. He was careful not to run in the same place where the arsonist had walked. He didn't want to disturb any footprints or other evidence.

The arson investigator was fast, but Pete was faster. He reached the curb at the far side of the lot behind the Morrises', then sat down to wait for the investigator. He dropped the tape.

"You scamp," the man said as he picked up the piece of tape. "You just want to play, don't you?"

The man stuffed the tape in his pocket then turned to go back.

"Open your eyes!" Pete shrieked. "Look around!"

The man glanced over his shoulder. "What's wrong with you now?" he asked.

Pete trotted toward the gas can.

"Hey, Allen!" the man shouted. "Come here and bring the fingerprint kit. I found a gas can!"

Pete watched while the two men dusted the gas can for fingerprints. He washed his whiskers while they put it in a plastic bag and labeled it. He saw them carefully walk through the weeds, noting where some were trampled.

Finally, satisfied that the fire investigators had discovered everything he wanted them to see, Pete sauntered back to their car, jumped inside, and finished off the ham sandwich.

Then he needed a nap. His stomach bulged from the sandwich, and he was tired from all the excitement, but he didn't want to go home yet. Once he went inside, Alex might not let him out again, so he crawled under the Kendrills' back porch, curled up in the dirt, and fell asleep.

11

*P*ete awoke to hear Alex calling him: "Here, Pete. Here, Pete. Time to come home."

Pete arched his back, stretched his hind legs, then stretched his front legs. He waited until Alex quit calling. When he heard Alex close the door, he came out from under the porch.

Pink clouds hovered at the horizon, chasing the setting sun. My favorite time of day, Pete thought. Mouse time.

He walked away from his house, across the backyard, and through the small grove of trees that separated the Kendrills' property from the lot behind theirs. He planned to return to the place where he had found the gas can. He didn't expect to discover any more clues; he was only curious to know what smells would remain from the investigators and their fingerprint dust.

Pete walked slowly, enjoying his freedom. He listened for any rustling in the long grass where an unsuspecting mouse might be caught unaware.

When he emerged from the weeds, he had reached the curb at the far side of the back lot. He stopped, then looked both ways.

To his left, at the curve of the dead-end street, a parked car hugged the curb in front of one of the vacant houses. It looked like the same car that the arsonist had used the night before.

Pete backed into the weeds, then crouched, making himself as inconspicuous as possible. Only his face peered out, staring through the dim light at the parked car and the three houses beyond it.

Soon he saw a person come around the side of the center house. Pete was too far away to tell if it was the same man who had started the fire at the Morrises' house.

The person walked slowly around the perimeter of the house. Pete's tail swished. His ears flattened. The faint scent of gasoline floated past him on the breeze.

He's going to do it again, Pete realized. It is the same man, and he's starting another house fire.

Pete raced for home, skimming the tops of the weeds, stretching his legs out as far as they would go. He ran up the back steps, pawed at the kitchen door, and called, "Alex! Come quick!"

Mrs. Kendrill opened the door, holding a mixing bowl in one hand and a spoon in the other. "There you are," she said. "We've been calling you."

She held the door open, but Pete did not go in.

"Hurry," he said. "Follow me!"

"Pete, get in here," Mrs. Kendrill said. She stepped out and tried to nudge him with her foot in the direction of the door.

Pete backed away.

"Alex is out looking for you," Mrs. Kendrill said. She set the bowl on the clothes dryer and tried to grab Pete.

He jumped out of her reach.

Mrs. Kendrill sighed, went in, and closed the door.

"Where is he?" Pete said. "Where's Alex?"

The door opened again. "Do you want to come in or don't you?" Mrs. Kendrill said.

Pete did not move. "I want Alex."

"Honestly," Mrs. Kendrill said. "I think you just like to hear yourself meow." She shut the door.

Pete heard the lock click. He hurried to the front of the house; maybe Alex was looking for him there.

"Here, Pete. Here, Pete." Alex turned the corner from Valley View Drive to Maple Street. He didn't think Pete would wander this far, but he wasn't sure. Maybe Pete had been so excited to be off the leash that he had gone too far.

Movement on the other side of the street caught Alex's attention. He stopped. Two people were walking in the same direction as Alex. Maybe they had seen Pete. He walked faster, trying to see who it was before he called out to them.

One of them laughed, and Alex stopped. Duke! Who was with him? The second person was too tall to be Henry. Maybe it was Duke's older brother, the one who had said his dog would eat Pete.

Alex remembered Duke's taunt: "Trouble always comes in threes." Was Duke making sure something else bad happened in Valley View Estates?

Maybe Duke did cut down the street signs and start the fire, Alex thought. Maybe I should have told Mom and Dad that I suspected him.

Duke and his companion got in a parked car. The engine started; lights came on.

Alex squatted on the sidewalk, hoping Duke wouldn't see him.

The car sped past. Duke's brother—the same one who had been with Duke before—was driving.

Alex watched the car turn the corner onto Valley View Drive. Instead of continuing down Maple Street, Alex turned and hurried home, calling Pete as he went.

I don't like not knowing where Pete is, Alex thought. There are too many dangers: cars, big dogs, unknown people. What would Duke and his companion have done if they had seen Pete? Maybe nothing; maybe something cruel.

Benjie met Alex at the door. "A big helicopter flew over," he said, "and dropped pieces of paper into our yard." He handed Alex a crayon drawing of green-and-red-striped cows. "It's a secret message," Benjie said, "about cows who give peppermint-flavored milk."

"Has Pete come home?" Alex asked. After seeing Duke just a block away, Alex was too nervous to go along with Benjie's game.

"Yes," Mrs. Kendrill said, "but he wouldn't come in. He just sat on the back porch and yowled. I think he's still out there."

Alex opened the back door and switched on the light.

"It's about time you came," Pete said. Then he bolted down the steps.

"You'd better catch him," Mrs. Kendrill said. "He wouldn't let me get near him."

"Come on, Pete," Alex said. "Time for dinner."

"You can't bribe me with food," Pete said. "I have something important to show you." He trotted across the backyard, pausing every few feet to make sure Alex was still in pursuit.

Each time, he waited until Alex was almost close enough to reach him before he hurried farther away.

Pete was nearly to Alder Court when Alex stopped.

"I'm not chasing you all over the neighborhood," Alex said. "You'd better come home with me or you'll be back on your leash tomorrow."

Leash. Pete growled at that dreaded word. He hesitated, knowing he could allow himself to be picked up and carried home, and no one would ever suspect that he held the key to an unsolved case of arson.

Pete decided not to give in. He was a cat of honor, and it was important for Alex to see what he had seen, even if it meant Pete lost his freedom for a few days.

"Just a few yards farther," Pete said. He trotted on.

"Okay," Alex said. "Stay out all night, if you want to. I'm going home. Just don't come howling around after I go to bed because I'm not getting up to let you in."

Alex turned around and started toward home.

This calls for drastic action, Pete thought. He remembered the one time he had fought with another cat. Several years ago an orange striped cat had come into Pete's yard, and Pete had bravely defended his property.

Pete had a nick in one ear where the orange cat had taken a bite out of him. When the orange cat bit his ear, Pete had screamed a bloodcurdling scream that he had never made before or since. The Kendrills, and several of their neighbors, had come running.

As Pete watched Alex walk away from him, toward home, he sat back on his haunches, tipped his face to the sky, and let loose. "Yeeeooowwww!" he shrieked.

Alex whirled around and ran toward him.

Pete got set to shriek again, but before he could do it, Alex reached him, scooped him up, and held him tight.

"I thought you'd been attacked by a dog," Alex said, "or maybe even a cougar."

Alex decided that from then on, Pete would be an indoor cat unless he was on the leash.

"I didn't mean it when I said I'd leave you out all night," Alex said. "I would never do that. I was only trying to persuade you to come with me."

"*Poof!*" The sound came from the end of the street.

Alex turned to look. A faint light flickered from the center house.

"Oh, no," he whispered. "There's another fire."

12

Alex saw a dark figure silhouetted against the rising flames. The figure hurried to a parked car, then put something in the trunk. The arsonist!

Alex turned to run home to call 911, then stopped. Should he call the fire department, or should he stay and try to get a license number from the car first?

It was important to call for help as soon as possible; he had seen how quickly a fire could damage a home. Still, the burning gray house and the houses on either side of it were all vacant, so there wasn't any chance of people being hurt. If Alex stayed and got a license-plate number, the police would probably catch the arsonist before he could start more fires.

Still clutching Pete, Alex knelt in the weeds.

The arsonist got in the car and drove away from the fire. As the car approached Alex and Pete, Alex tried to read the license number, but the headlights shone in his eyes. He would have to wait until the car passed him, then try to see the number on the back license plate.

The car accelerated as it went by. Alex tried to see but he got only the first two numbers: 2–4. That wouldn't be enough.

He stood and ran after the car, squinting at the back plate.

2–4–4–K–X–something. He didn't get the last letter, but he thought he had the rest of it right: 2–4–4–K–X. He repeated it aloud, wishing he had something to write on.

The fire burned higher, lighting up the land around it.

Tires squealed; red brake lights glowed. *Pete buried his face in the crook of Alex's elbow.* The car roared in reverse back down the street toward Alex.

He's seen me, Alex realized. He must have looked in the rearview mirror.

Alex took off toward home. He was halfway to the grove of trees when a gunshot sounded behind him. Alex hit the ground. *He let go of Pete, who ran to the closest tree and climbed it.*

"Hold it right there," the man called as he ran toward Alex. "Don't say anything. Don't yell for help. I missed you on purpose the first time, but I won't miss again."

A chill prickled Alex's arms. He recognized that voice. Mr. Woolsey, the man who had built all the houses in Valley View Estates, was the arsonist!

Alex stayed sprawled in the weeds as Mr. Woolsey approached.

From the far side of the trees, Alex heard his mother's voice calling, "Alex? Alex, where are you?" Maybe she heard the shot, he thought. If I don't come, she'll know something's wrong.

The man approached Alex. "Stand up," he said softly. "Keep your hands over your head while you get in my car."

"Alex?" Mrs. Kendrill's voice rang out. "Al-ex!"

"Don't answer," Mr. Woolsey said. "Don't say anything."

Alex stood, then walked to the car.

The fire raged around the entire house now. When his parents came looking for him, they would see the flames and call 911, but they wouldn't know Alex had been abducted.

Just before he got in the car, Alex slipped his watch off his wrist and let it drop to the street. He pretended to cough, to cover up the sound that the watch made when it hit the pavement.

Mr. Woolsey slid behind the wheel, slammed the door shut, then took off so fast the tires squealed again.

Good, Alex thought. Make some noise. Call attention to this car.

"Why did you set fire to that house?" Alex asked.

"I didn't set any fire. I just happened to drive by and

saw smoke. I was on my way to call the fire department when I spotted you."

Alex said nothing. He knew Mr. Woolsey was lying, but it didn't seem smart to argue with someone holding a gun.

"You're the one who set the fire," Mr. Woolsey said. "That's why I came after you."

"Me? That isn't true. I had nothing to do with either of the fires."

"Kids these days can't be trusted. It's lucky I saw you there in the street, or you would probably have set more houses on fire."

Alex stared at Mr. Woolsey. Was he really going to try to put the blame on Alex? If so, would anyone believe him?

Maybe they would. After all, why would Mr. Woolsey destroy homes that his company had built—houses that he owned?

"I'm the one who called the fire department last night," Alex said. "I wouldn't do that if I had set the fire."

"You might. Some people start fires because they like the excitement of having the fire trucks come."

"And some people start fires so they can collect the insurance money," Alex said. He hadn't intended to say that. He blurted it out the minute he had the thought, because he knew it was a motive for Mr. Woolsey's actions.

Most of the houses in Valley View Estates had not sold yet. Maybe Mr. Woolsey was having money trouble; maybe he owed a bank for some construction loans and now, because the houses had not sold, he couldn't make the payments.

As soon as Alex accused Mr. Woolsey, he knew he should not have done so. Mr. Woolsey had looked nervous when they first got in the car. Now he seemed angry. One hand gripped the steering wheel while the other held the handgun. When he glanced at Alex, his eyes were cold, dark marbles.

"Where are you taking me?" Alex asked.

"Be quiet. I'm trying to think."

Alex said nothing more. He hoped his parents would waste no time calling the police. They would know something was terribly wrong when Alex didn't return, especially if Pete went home.

But would Pete go home? Maybe Pete would stay in the tree and howl until Dad brought a ladder out there. That might not happen until tomorrow morning.

Too bad Pete can't talk, Alex thought. He saw the car, just as plainly as I did, and he heard me repeat the license-plate number. Maybe he even recognized Mr. Woolsey.

Alex wondered if Pete had purposely led him to the scene of the second arson. Had Pete been there earlier and seen Mr. Woolsey? Had Pete run away from Alex as a way to make Alex follow him and discover what was happening?

No, Alex thought. Don't let your imagination run wild. Even if Pete did see what Mr. Woolsey was up to, it wouldn't mean anything to him.

Pete's a fine cat, but that's all he is, just a cat. He certainly is not a detective.

13

Two blocks from the fire, Mr. Woolsey's foot stomped on the brake pedal.

Alex's head jerked forward at the sudden stop. He gripped the edge of his seat as the car made a fast U-turn, roared back to the dead-end street, and screeched to a stop in front of the burning building.

Mr. Woolsey got out, walked to the rear of the car, and opened the trunk.

Alex looked hopefully in all directions but saw no one. Surely his parents would have seen the fire by now, especially if they were outside looking for him. He wondered if they were waiting at home for the fire trucks to arrive.

The door beside Alex opened.

"Get out."

Alex looked at the handgun, which was pointed directly at him. He got out of the car.

"This way." Mr. Woolsey motioned with his head toward the tan house to the right of the fire.

Alex saw that Mr. Woolsey now held a length of rope in his other hand. He's going to tie me up, Alex realized, and leave me in the second house.

"Go faster. Run!"

Alex jogged toward the empty building, with Mr. Woolsey directly behind him.

The first fire roared upward, almost to the roof. A dark, dense fog of smoke surged into the night sky.

I can't let him do this, Alex thought. He'll tie me and leave me there, and then—the realization made Alex's stomach lurch—and then he'll set fire to that house, too.

He's gambling that I won't be found until it's too late. He'll blame the fires on me after I'm dead. I'm the only one who knows who the true arsonist is, so if he blames me and I'm not here to defend myself, he'll get away with it.

"Don't yell for help, and don't try to escape," Mr. Woolsey said. "This gun is loaded, and I'm an excellent shot. I'll say I caught you starting the fire and that I fired when you ran away. I'll say I couldn't tell who it was."

Would anyone believe that? Alex wondered. Did it matter? He would be dead whether anyone believed Mr. Woolsey's story or not.

Mr. Woolsey used a key to unlock the tan house. He pushed the door open. "Get inside."

Alex stepped into the dark interior. Dim light from the

burning building next door gleamed through the dining-room window to his left.

"This way," Mr. Woolsey said, shoving Alex forward until they reached an open bathroom door.

"Put your hands on the wall," Mr. Woolsey said.

Alex hesitated. Should he do as he was told and hope that help would come in time? Or should he bolt, taking a chance that Mr. Woolsey's shot might miss him, and that he could hide or get away?

"Now!" Mr. Woolsey said.

Reluctantly, Alex put his palms against the wallboard. He couldn't run for it when Mr. Woolsey was so close. Even a poor shot could hit a target that was in the same room.

Mr. Woolsey bound Alex's feet with the rope.

"Put your hands behind you."

Mr. Woolsey tied Alex's wrists together behind his back, pulling the rope tight. "Now hop into the bathroom."

With short, jerky jumps Alex crossed the threshold into the small bathroom.

Mr. Woolsey stood with his hand on the doorknob. "I'm sorry I have to do this," he said, "but you shouldn't have been sneaking around in the dark."

"I wasn't sneaking. I was trying to catch my cat."

"I wish I had a choice, but I'm in it too deep to turn back now."

"You'll get caught," Alex said, "even without me. My parents know I wouldn't commit arson, and they know I was home with them when the first fire started. They'll pursue this. You'll be arrested."

Mr. Woolsey pulled the bathroom door closed. Alex heard the doorknob jiggling and realized Mr. Woolsey was doing something to it from the other side so that the door wouldn't open.

Alex heard Mr. Woolsey run toward the front door. He made himself stay quiet. As soon as Mr. Woolsey was gone, Alex would yell for help. He didn't want to call out too soon, for fear Mr. Woolsey would come back and fire the gun through the bathroom door.

Alex knew that his parents or one of the other families in Valley View Estates would see the fire soon, if they hadn't already, and that fire trucks would arrive.

He hoped that the firefighters would hear his shouts. If they didn't . . . No. Alex wouldn't let himself think about what would happen if they didn't hear him.

Alex leaned against the door, straining to hear when Mr. Woolsey's car drove off. Instead he heard the footsteps again, this time running toward the bathroom door.

For an instant, hope flared. Had guilt changed Mr. Woolsey's mind? Was he going to untie Alex and let him go?

Wishful thinking turned to dread as the smell of gasoline seeped under the door. Footsteps ran away; the front door slammed shut.

Because the other two fires had been started around the perimeters of the houses, Alex had assumed Mr. Woolsey would do that again, and that it would take some time for the flames to reach this bathroom. Instead Mr. Woolsey had poured gasoline inside the house, next to where Alex was confined.

He heard a muffled curse from outside the bathroom window, followed by the sound of something hitting the wall.

Alex sat on the edge of the bathtub, swung his legs up and over the side, then stood in the tub and peeked out the window.

Mr. Woolsey was pounding on the wall with his gasoline container, trying to shake out a few more drops. Mr. Woolsey had not intended to start a second fire tonight; maybe he had emptied the container at the gray house, and now there wasn't enough gasoline left to set fire to the tan house.

He saw Mr. Woolsey strike a match, then toss it toward the base of the house. Alex couldn't see if anything caught fire, but Mr. Woolsey gave a satisfied nod, then ran off.

Alex stood helplessly in the bathtub, listening for the sound of sirens.

Minutes later, fingers of flame gripped the bottom edge of the door, then crawled upward.

Water, Alex thought. I'm in a bathroom. If I can turn on the water, I can stay wet, and keep my clothes from catching fire. He sat down in the tub, facing away from the faucet.

He scooted backward until his hands touched the front of the tub. He groped for the faucet, found it, and turned it. Nothing happened. He yanked it as far as it would go; still nothing.

The main water valve to the house must not be open. Probably the water didn't get turned on until people were ready to move in.

Thick smoke oozed under the door and rose, curling around Alex's head. He looked at the small window over the tub. He could probably squeeze through it if he could get it open, but with his hands tied behind him, he couldn't reach the latch, and there was nothing in the bathroom that he could stand on.

"Help!" Alex screamed. He hadn't heard any fire trucks arrive, so he didn't think anyone was near enough to hear him, but he shouted anyway. "Help! I'm trapped in here!"

14

Pete flattened himself on the tree limb. He watched as the man approached Alex. He saw Alex get in the man's car. He watched the taillights disappear down the street.

Pete clung to the branch and howled. In his terror at the sound of the gunshot, he had climbed higher than he had ever gone before. The branch beneath him, already bent downward from Pete's weight, dipped lower when he tried to turn around.

Behind him, he heard Mr. and Mrs. Kendrill call Alex's name again and again.

"Out here!" Pete shrieked. "Come out here and look. There's another fire!"

But the people did not come. He would have to climb down by himself.

The branch was too narrow for him to turn around on, so Pete backed cautiously toward the tree trunk, his claws digging into the bark. He had gone only a few feet when he

*saw headlights race toward the burning house. Pete lay mo-
tionless, his blue eyes wide.*

*Peering through the leaves, Pete saw the man take rope
from the trunk. He saw Alex get out of the car, then run toward the tan house. The man followed him inside.*

*Soon the man came out alone, without the rope. He got
a gasoline can from his car. He ran inside the house, then
returned and went to the rear of the building. Pete couldn't
see him then, but he knew what the gasoline was for.*

*Alex is in there! Pete thought. He hasn't come out. That
horrid man is starting another fire, and this time Alex is inside the house.*

*Hoping that the man would not see his white fur, Pete
backed quickly toward the tree trunk. In his haste, he was
not as cautious as he should have been, and his hind feet
slipped off the narrow branch.*

*Pete dangled, his body swinging in the air as his front
claws dug desperately into the branch.*

*He managed to hang on while he swung one hind foot
and then the other far enough up to get a grip.*

*When all his paws were back on the branch, he stretched
out as low as he could get and waited for his heart to quit
racing. That had been close. Too close.*

*Pete peered downward, stunned by his narrow escape.
The ground seemed so far away that it made him dizzy to
look.*

Humans were fond of saying that a cat always lands on

all four feet, and most of the time that was true, but if a cat fell by mistake from this height, the cat would be in bad shape, no matter how it landed.

Pete yearned to stay still, and wait for Mr. Kendrill to bring a ladder from the house, and climb up, and carry him to safety—but he couldn't stay in the tree and wait to be rescued. He had to help Alex.

Pete concentrated on feeling his way along the branch, making sure each paw was in a stable spot before he put his weight on it. He finally reached the trunk of the tree, where he was able to turn around. He yelled for help, feeling more secure now that he was off that wiggly branch.

"Come this way!" he yowled. "Alex is in the burning house!"

Where were his people? Why didn't they come looking for him and Alex?

His cries brought no response, and Pete knew he could not wait any longer to be rescued. Gripping the tree trunk with his paws, he lowered his head and started down the tree face first. Quickly, before he lost his courage, he half slid, half climbed down the tree trunk.

Six feet above the ground, he let go with his front paws and shoved off with his hind feet, leaping into the tall grass. Even before he landed, his legs were running toward home. Behind him, he heard the car drive off again.

Pete raced past the rest of the trees, moving faster than

he had ever run before. He leaped onto the back porch, already shouting for help.

"Come out!" Pete cried. "Alex needs help!"

The door opened immediately.

"Pete's back," Mrs. Kendrill said. She called out, "Alex? Alex, come home. Pete's here!"

She held the door, but Pete turned and ran down the steps.

"Pete!" It was Mr. Kendrill this time. "Bad cat! Come back here."

"Something isn't right," Mrs. Kendrill said. "It's after eight o'clock. Alex wouldn't just take off like this in the dark, without telling us."

Pete crept back toward the porch, staying far enough away that he could escape a quick lunge toward him.

Alex's parents looked at each other for a moment.

"Let's catch Pete, since he's here," Mr. Kendrill said. "Then we'll look for Alex. I'm sure he's just walking around calling the cat, but I'll feel easier when he's home."

Mrs. Kendrill grabbed a flashlight. "We'll be back in a minute, Benjie," she called.

"I'm coming, too," Benjie replied as he ran after his parents. "Maybe the red-white-and-blue monster monkeys have kidnapped Alex. They wear costumes to make it look as if they're patriotic citizens, but underneath they're

wicked and they steal children and turn them into garbage cans. Or maybe the silver snakes from Saturn have
come to Earth disguised as ribbons and Alex had one tied
on a present, and when he untied it, it bit him and spit
poison up his nose."

For once, Mr. and Mrs. Kendrill paid no attention to
Benjie's chatter. Instead they followed Pete across the
back lot and into the maple grove.

Firelight flickered beyond the trees.

"Look!" Mrs. Kendrill said. "There's another fire! It's
one of the vacant houses."

"I'll go back and call the fire department," Mr. Kendrill
said. "You see if you can catch Pete."

"*Call the police, too!*" Pete screeched. "*Rescue Alex!
He's still inside one of the houses.*"

"Good boy," Mrs. Kendrill said. "Stay still, and let me
pick you up." She moved slowly toward the cat.

*Pete longed to sit quietly while Mrs. Kendrill approached
him; he wanted to allow her to carry him home where it was
safe. He wanted to hunker over his crunchies for a bedtime
snack and then stretch out on the carpet and wash his
whiskers. Even more, he wanted to lie on Alex's bed and get
a cat massage.*

*But he couldn't go home. Not yet. Not when Alex was in-
side a burning house. Somehow he had to let the people
know where Alex was.*

He sat as still as a stuffed toy cat while Mrs. Kendrill came closer.

"Good boy," she murmured. "Good Pete. No wonder you're skittery, with houses burning down all around us. I'm going to take you home and give you some kitty num-num."

Pete's tail twitched. Kitty num-num was his favorite treat in the whole world. It came in a small can and tasted of tuna and whitefish. Usually Pete got kitty num-num only on Christmas or when Alex decided it was time to celebrate Pete's birthday. (No one, not even Pete himself, knew what date he had been born, so Alex had chosen an approximate date, and then sometime during that week each year, whenever it was convenient, he made a fuss over Pete, singing "Happy Birthday" and feeding him treats.)

Pete waited until Mrs. Kendrill bent over to grab him, then he bolted toward the house where Alex was held captive.

"Hold still, Pete!" Mrs. Kendrill said. "There will be loud sirens and trucks and people here soon, and they'll scare the fur off you. Now come back here and let me take you home."

Pete backed toward the tan house. From inside it, he heard Alex's voice: "Help! Somebody please help me!"

Pete looked to see if Mrs. Kendrill had heard, but she continued to scowl at Pete as she approached. Humans don't hear as well as cats do—more proof of the superiority of cats. He would have to go closer to the burning building.

He felt the heat from the flames; he heard the crackling sound of wood splintering. Thick smoke billowed around him, making it hard to breathe and even harder to see where he was going. Pete's heart thudded as if he were being chased by a Doberman, but he moved closer to the fire.

A siren rose and fell in the distance, getting louder. Mrs. Kendrill stopped pursuing Pete; she ran toward the intersection of Alder Court and Valley View Drive. "This way!" she cried, waving her arms as she came to the corner. "This way!"

The fire engine slowed just enough to turn the corner, then raced to the end of the street. Shouts filled the night air as the three firefighters, wearing bright yellow slickers, leaped down.

Trembling with fear, Pete watched them approach. He hated loud noises and quick movements. At any other time of his life, he would have streaked for home at even a hint of such commotion.

This night, he stayed where he was. Dwarfed by the tower of flame behind him and the huge equipment before him, Pete arched his back, stood all his fur on end, and opened his mouth wide.

"Over here!" he screeched. "Come to this house first. Alex is inside!"

His cries were drowned out by the shouting firefighters and water gushing from the hoses.

"Pete! Here, Petey, Petey."

Pete blinked and squinted into the smoke toward Benjie's voice. He saw Benjie running toward him.

"Hey, kid! Get away from there!" One of the firefighters had spotted Benjie, too.

"I have to get our cat," Benjie yelled.

"No! It isn't safe!"

Benjie kept going.

Pete backed farther away from him.

15

Rocky walked around the exterior of his new house, but it was too dark to see anything. He wished he had a flashlight so he could shine it in the windows. He glanced at his watch: 8:15. Where was Mrs. Woolsey?

"She must have forgotten," Blake said. "Let's go back to the motel; I'll call her and set a time for tomorrow morning."

As Blake and Rocky started toward their car, a car drove up and a man jumped out and hurried toward them. "I'm Thurgood Woolsey," he said. "Sorry you had to wait." He sounded out of breath, as if he had been running. "My wife was detained, and I didn't know about this appointment. She just called me."

He kept looking over his shoulder, as if someone were following him.

"Did the arson squad learn anything?" Blake asked.

"What?" Mr. Woolsey looked as if he didn't know what Blake was talking about. "Oh. Oh, that. I haven't talked to them. I haven't been home."

"I didn't hear from them today either," Blake said.

"Can we go inside?" Rocky asked. "I want to see my room."

Mr. Woolsey fumbled in his pockets. "Oh. I don't have the key to this house. Can you wait while I drive to my office to get it? It's only a few blocks away."

"Why don't I follow you," Blake said, "and get the keys. That way you won't have to come back here."

"Good idea," Mr. Woolsey said. "Yes, I won't have to come back here. Let's go, then." He got in his car and, without waiting for Blake to follow, took off.

"It's a good thing I know where his office is," Blake said as Mr. Woolsey's car sped away.

"Is it okay if I wait here?" Rocky asked. "It's such a nice night; I'd rather walk around than go to Mr. Woolsey's office."

"Stay close by," Blake said. "I'll be back in ten minutes." He got in his car and left.

Rocky walked to the corner, then turned left intending to walk to Elm Lane, the street where he had lived for six days. He was curious to see what the burned house looked like in the dark. Before he got to Elm, he heard a siren approaching.

Rocky listened as the sound came closer. He could tell when the vehicle turned off the main road and entered Valley View Estates.

Was it a police car? Rocky's stomach twisted into a knot. Had last night's fire been traced to the mob who smuggled drugs, the mob whose leader Rocky's mom had testified against? Were the police chasing Mafia members, men who were after Blake and Rocky?

Don't be paranoid, he told himself. But it was hard not to be when he knew his life was threatened.

A fire truck roared into view, then turned down Alder Court.

Not another fire! Rocky thought. Which house this time?

He ran after the truck and soon saw the leaping flames. It was like having a terrible nightmare repeat itself two nights in a row.

Rocky saw three firefighters jump from the truck, unroll their hoses, and attach them to a bright red fire hydrant that squatted at the end of the street. The hoses expanded like giant boa constrictors as the water coursed through them.

He saw Mr. and Mrs. Kendrill on the far side of the street, watching. Alder Court was just one block over from Elm Lane; they must have seen the fire from their backyard and called the fire department. He wondered where Alex and Benjie were.

Rocky saw that it wasn't just one house on fire this time, it was two. The gray house was fully aflame, the tan house much less so. A third house, to the left of the gray one, seemed okay.

Mr. Kendrill ran toward one of the firefighters, shouting, "All three houses are vacant! It's new construction that hasn't sold yet."

That firefighter quickly alerted the others that none of the property was occupied.

The firefighters split up, with two of them concentrating on the left side of the gray house, apparently to keep the flames from spreading to the third building. The other firefighter sprayed water on the front side of the tan house.

Rocky stayed in the trees on the uncleared land across the street from where the Kendrills stood. If they saw him, they would ask if his family had found a place to live, and then he'd have to tell them which house he was going to move into.

He planned to stay away from Alex and Benjie in the future. Eventually, Alex would find out where Rocky lived, but by then he would have caught on that Rocky did not intend to become friends.

As Rocky watched the great hoses spew water onto the flames, something bright red caught his eye. Squinting through the smoky haze, Rocky saw Benjie, wearing a red jacket, running toward the burning houses.

He heard a firefighter yell at Benjie to go back, but the little boy kept going. Rocky had talked to Benjie only twice; both times Benjie had told him a wild story about Martians and a yellow dragon that ate naughty children. Was Benjie acting out one of his imaginative stories? If so, he was playing with danger.

Rocky was closer to Benjie than any of the firefighters were. He took off toward the boy. As he got closer, he saw that Benjie was chasing Alex's cat.

He couldn't believe that the cat would go toward a burning building that way. Usually an animal's natural fear of fire would send it streaking in the opposite direction. But the fool cat kept going closer, yowling like crazy, while Benjie tried to catch him.

"Get back, you kids!" the firefighter hollered. "Both of you!"

Rocky realized the man meant him as well as Benjie. He stopped. "Benjie!" he yelled. "Come this way! Come with me!"

"I can't! I have to save Pete!"

"Pete can save himself," Rocky shouted. "He'll run to safety if you leave him alone."

"Follow me," Pete yelled as he turned the corner to the back side of the house. "Come this way!"

"Help!" Alex screamed. "I'm inside! Help!"

"Listen!" Pete screeched. "Don't you hear him?"

His fur felt scorched, and every time he yowled, the

smoke burned his throat. What was wrong with the humans? Why didn't they hear Alex?

Benjie lunged for Pete, tripped, and fell on his face. He lay, crying, on the ground, his breath coming in great gulps.

Pete watched the firefighter who had yelled at Benjie run to the boy. Pete backed away from Benjie. It took all his willpower to stay quiet, but he wanted the fireman to hear Alex.

The fireman reached Benjie, bent down, and lifted the crying boy over his shoulder like a sack of potatoes.

"You could have been killed, running at a burning building that way," the fireman said. He carried Benjie toward the street, where Mr. Kendrill met him. The fireman handed the boy to his father, then returned to his duties without saying a word.

Pete stared at the people. What could he do to make them come after him? They had to come this way, to the back side of the house, to hear Alex.

Pete's eyes and nose filled with smoke. He coughed. When he inhaled, he felt the hot smoke fill his chest. Panic-stricken, he stood in the weeds, listening for Alex's voice.

Above him, a piece of cedar siding ignited, broke free from the house, and dropped.

Pete did not see it coming. The burning wood landed with a sickening thud on the back of his head.

Pete crumpled. He lay motionless with the burning wood across his neck.

16

Sweat dripped from Alex's face. His voice grew hoarse from shouting, the inside of his nose hurt from inhaling the smoke, and his eyeballs felt scorched.

Alex heard the voices of the firefighters outside, and once he thought he heard Benjie calling Pete, but nobody heard his rasping cries.

Pieces of flaming wallboard broke free and fell around him, hitting the ceramic bathtub. The light fixture, its wires melted, crashed into the sink. So far nothing had hit him, but Alex knew he couldn't escape the falling pieces much longer.

He lay down in the bathtub, then rolled onto his stomach. If parts of the burning house dropped on him, and his clothes caught on fire, he planned to roll from his stomach to his back, and then to his stomach again. He would keep rolling, over and over, to put out the flames.

But what if his hair caught fire? What if so much

burning debris dropped into the tub that he had no place left to roll?

If they don't rescue me soon, Alex thought, I'm a goner. "Help!" he cried, forcing his voice, even though his throat throbbed and his cries were more squeak than shout. "Somebody, please help me!"

A wooden towel bar caught fire, fell off the wall, and landed on Alex's arms. He gasped as the flames singed his skin. His hands jerked upward, throwing the towel bar off his arms. He rolled over, sat up, and kicked the towel bar to the end of the tub, where it smoldered like a small log in a fireplace.

When Alex tried to yell again, he coughed instead. He was breathing too much smoke, but there wasn't anything he could do about it.

He sat in the bathtub, coughing, choking on smoke. A wall of fire engulfed the bathroom door. The outside wall beside the tub burned high now, too. Even if his feet weren't tied, even if he could run, there was no place to go except into the blaze.

Across the street, Mr. Kendrill scolded Benjie. "You scared the life out of us, running toward a fire that way. Where was your brain?"

"Pete's over there," Benjie sobbed. "Pete's going to get burned up in the fire."

"Pete will run away from the fire," Mr. Kendrill said. "He'll take care of himself."

"Rocky's over there, too. He yelled at me to go with him."

"Rocky Morris?" Mr. Kendrill said.

"I'll bet he set this fire, too," Benjie said. "I told you he was bad."

"I wonder if the Morrises have moved into one of the other vacant houses," Mr. Kendrill said.

Mrs. Kendrill said, "It's odd that Alex hasn't returned. He wouldn't go out of our neighborhood to look for Pete, and surely he heard the fire truck."

"Maybe he came home but doesn't know where we are. We'd better check."

"Come on, Benjie," Mrs. Kendrill said.

"I want to stay here and watch the fire," Benjie said.

"You're coming with us," Mrs. Kendrill replied. "You can't be trusted to stay put."

Benjie followed his parents away from the excitement. He walked on the edge of the curb, pretending it was a tightrope stretched high in the air above a pool teeming with bright green sharks. Their gold teeth glittered as they snapped at his feet.

Something caught Benjie's attention. Forgetting the sharks, he stepped into the street.

"Mom! Dad!" he called. "I found Alex's watch."

He ran to catch up with his parents, then held out the watch. "It was lying in the street."

"If Alex isn't in the house," Mr. Kendrill said, "we'll drive around the neighborhood."

"If we don't find him right away," Mrs. Kendrill said, "I'm calling the police."

A second fire truck roared up. The firefighters rushed toward the tan house.

Rocky continued to watch the fire, puzzling over the odd behavior of Alex's cat. He walked along the edge of the trees until he could see the back side of the house, where Pete had gone. He got there just in time to see a flaming board fall from the house and land on top of Pete. The cat lay still.

Rocky rushed toward Pete, stripping off his shirt as he ran.

He smelled burned fur even before he reached the cat. Rocky kicked the blazing board off Pete, then dropped to his knees beside the motionless brown-and-white body. He threw his shirt over Pete, patted it to put out the flames, then tossed the shirt aside.

Looking closely, he saw that the cat's collar was burned through, and his fur was scorched, but the skin did not appear badly burned.

Pete's eyes remained closed, and Rocky could not tell

if the cat was still breathing. How do you feel a cat's pulse? he wondered.

Rocky and Nathan had taken a first-aid and CPR class as part of a Boy Scout training session, back when Rocky was still Clifford, so he knew how to help a person who had stopped breathing, but he wasn't sure how to help a cat.

I have to try, he thought. The memory of Alex stroking Pete's fur while he said, "Pete is the best friend I have," flashed into Rocky's mind. Alex loves his cat as much as I loved my dog; I can't let Pete die.

Maybe he could do artificial breathing on a cat, the same way it was done on a person.

Knowing he had nothing to lose, Rocky opened Pete's mouth and made sure there wasn't anything in it. He put his thumb and forefinger on the small pink tongue and pulled it forward so Pete wouldn't choke on it. He closed Pete's mouth.

Rocky took a deep breath, leaned his face close to Pete's, and put his mouth over the cat's nose. Gently he blew a puff of air into Pete's nostrils. As he did, he placed his hands on Pete's side; he felt the cat's chest expand as the air entered his lungs. Rocky lifted his mouth, inhaled, then blew into Pete's nose again.

Each time he blew, the cat's chest rose, then fell back when Rocky removed his mouth. He waited four seconds in between each puff. Inhale, blow. One-two-three-four. Inhale, blow. One-two-three-four.

After blowing seven times, he felt Pete's side rise by itself before he blew the next puff of air. Rocky waited, keeping his hands on the cat's side. "Yes," he whispered. "Breathe by yourself."

Up, down, up, down. Pete's side rose and fell in a slow, steady rhythm.

"Yes!" Rocky said. Wait until I tell Nathan I used my Scout training on a cat, he thought—and immediately realized he could never tell Nathan.

Heat from the flames slapped at Rocky's face. He had to move Pete away from the fire.

Carefully, Rocky slid both hands under the still body, lifted it gently, and cradled it against him.

"Hang on, Pete," he whispered. "We'll get you to a vet right away, and you'll be home with Alex before you know it."

Holding Pete against his bare chest, Rocky stood up. As he started away from the fire, he heard a faint voice.

"Help!"

Shock sent tingles across Rocky's scalp and down his arms. That was Alex's voice, and it came from inside the burning house.

"Alex!" he yelled. "Where are you?"

The voice sounded weak and scratchy, like a car radio

when reception was bad. "In here!" it said, then started coughing.

Clutching Pete, Rocky ran to the front of the house.

The closest firefighter shouted, "Get back! Stay away!"

"Alex is inside!" Rocky yelled. "My friend is trapped in the house. I heard him call for help."

Three firefighters rushed to the back side of the house. "Help!"

"That small window," one of them said, pointing. "Probably a bathroom."

"We're going in," another said into her radio. "There's a child inside. Send an ambulance. Repeat: we're going in."

Rocky crossed the street. He knew he couldn't help Alex now, and it was important to help Pete. He carried the inert cat past the grove of trees and into the Kendrills' yard. Pete was breathing, but he still needed help. Fast.

Rocky pounded on the Kendrills' back door. Nobody answered. They're probably out looking for Alex, he thought.

He wasn't sure if he should wait there for the Kendrills to return, or if he should carry Pete back to his own new house. Blake would be there by now; he would drive Pete to a veterinarian.

Rocky started toward his new house, but he had gone only half a block when Blake drove up. The Kendrills were right behind him.

All of them jumped out when they saw Rocky carrying

Pete. Benjie burst into tears. "I knew Pete was going to die if I didn't catch him," he sobbed.

"Pete got too close to the fire," Rocky said, "and was knocked out by a piece of siding that fell."

"Have you seen Alex?" Mr. Kendrill asked.

"Alex is trapped in one of the burning houses," Rocky said.

The color drained from Mrs. Kendrill's face. "Alex?" she whispered. "Are you sure?"

"I heard him call for help while I was giving Pete mouth-to-nose resuscitation," Rocky said. "The firefighters have gone in to get him."

Mr. Kendrill ran toward the fire.

"The red-white-and-blue monster monkeys got Alex!" Benjie wailed. "They've fried him like toast, and they'll put jam on him and eat him for breakfast."

Mrs. Kendrill hesitated, looking at Benjie. "Hush now," she said. "We have to go. Alex needs help."

"Benjie can stay with us," Blake said. "We'll find a veterinarian for your cat, and then we'll come back here."

"Thank you," Mrs. Kendrill said. "There's an emergency veterinary clinic at the junction of Highway 50 and East Road."

Mrs. Kendrill rushed down the street after her husband.

"Get in my car, Benjie," Blake said softly. "Rocky and I need you to help with Pete."

"Will Alex be okay?" Benjie asked. "Can they get him out?"

"Alex will be fine," Rocky said. "Those firefighters know exactly what to do, and the house Alex was in wasn't burning as badly as the other house was." He tried to sound confident, but he wondered if Alex would survive such an inferno. Even if the firefighters could reach him, he would probably be badly burned.

I told the firefighters my friend was inside, Rocky thought, and it's true. I care about Alex; I want him to be okay.

Rocky got in the backseat so Benjie could sit beside him. He laid Pete across his lap, trying to move him as little as possible.

The little boy put his hand in front of Pete's nose, as if hoping the cat would recognize the smell.

"Wake up, Petey," Benjie pleaded. "Please wake up." Tears made wet paths through the smudges on Benjie's cheeks.

Rocky remembered his own tearful ride when he had left his dog behind forever. He hoped Pete would recover; he hoped Benjie would not have to say good-bye.

17

Alex heard shouts outside.

"In here!" he called. *Cough, cough, cough.* "I'm locked in!"

Water gushed from hoses that were now aimed at the outside bathroom wall. The flames hissed into steam as water cascaded over them.

At the same time, axes chopped at the burning bathroom door, splintering the charred wood.

Alex sat on the edge of the tub, his breathing shallow as he tried not to inhale more smoke. His eyes smarted; his throat felt raw; his arms throbbed where the towel bar had burned them.

Sparks erupted as pieces of the door hit the tile floor. Two firefighters pushed through at the same time. Alex stood and stumbled toward them.

"He's tied!" one of the them said. "It will be faster to carry him out."

One firefighter put his hands under Alex's arms; the second firefighter grasped his legs. Flames nipped their ankles as they carried him across the blazing living room.

Just as they went into the yard, the roof on the back side of the house caved in. Ceiling joists, trailing streamers of smoke and flame, collapsed to the floor. One landed directly in the bathtub.

Alex saw the roof fall. If he had still been in that bathtub, it would have landed on him, and no amount of rolling back and forth would have saved him.

The next few minutes blurred together. Someone untied his hands, then his feet. Someone else asked his name and phone number. He was helped onto a gurney and given oxygen. Medics took his pulse, looked in his mouth, and checked the severity of his burns.

The noises of the fire filled the night—wood crackling and splitting, water spraying, two-way radios giving and receiving instructions, people running and shouting.

Alex couldn't stop shaking.

One medic spread a blanket across him, keeping Alex's arms on top of it.

Alex's parents rushed to his side. Questions piled on top of each other: "Are you all right?" "What happened?" "What were you doing in that house?"

"He's in shock," the medic said, "and suffering from smoke inhalation and second-degree burns. Are you his parents?"

"Yes."

"We need to get him to the hospital."

"Of course. We'll follow you."

A police officer arrived and hurried to Alex's side as the gurney was lifted into the ambulance. "The medics said your hands and feet were tied when they found you," the officer said.

"Mr. Woolsey tied me," Alex rasped. "He started the fires."

"Mr. Woolsey?" Mrs. Kendrill said. "Are you sure?"

"I saw him do it," Alex said. "I couldn't tell who it was—*cough, cough*—so I tried to get his license number. He saw me, and shot at me, and made me go—" He stopped, overcome by a fit of coughing.

"He shot at you!" Mr. Kendrill said.

"Save your voice, son," the officer said. "You've told me enough for now." He turned to Mr. and Mrs. Kendrill. "Who is Mr. Woolsey?"

"Thurgood Woolsey, the man who built all of these houses."

The medics closed the ambulance door.

"His phone number is on the FOR SALE signs," Mr. Kendrill said, pointing. "We'll be at the hospital with Alex."

"I'll contact you later. I'll need to talk to Alex again, but it can wait."

Mr. and Mrs. Kendrill ran to their car. The ambulance

pulled out of Alder Court and headed down Valley View toward the highway into Seattle. The red lights and siren remained off.

One of the medics said, "Take deep breaths of the oxygen, Alex. Try to get that smoke cleared out of your body."

At the hospital emergency room, Alex received intravenous fluids and humidified oxygen. He finally quit shaking and coughing.

Small blisters puffed on the underside of his arms where the burning towel bar had landed. The skin under the blisters looked red and swollen.

"We'll keep you a couple of hours," the doctor said. "I don't want to put anything on your arms yet." He turned to Mr. and Mrs. Kendrill, who stood beside Alex's bed. "Much longer in that smoke, and your son would have had serious lung damage," he said. "He's lucky to be alive."

"Can you talk enough to tell us what happened?" Mr. Kendrill asked.

"I was trying to catch Pete," Alex said, "and he ran toward where Mr. Woolsey had set fire to the gray house." He gave a quick synopsis of the events that followed. "Did Pete come home?" he asked.

"Is Pete your brother?" asked the doctor.

"He's my cat."

"Pete got too close to the fire and was hit by a piece of

siding that fell," Mrs. Kendrill said. "Rocky heard you call for help when he tried to rescue Pete. He alerted the fire-fighters."

"Rocky saved my life," Alex said.

"He may have saved Pete, too," Mr. Kendrill added. "Pete was knocked unconscious; Rocky did mouth-to-nose resuscitation to revive him, and now Mr. Morris is taking Pete to the emergency veterinary clinic."

"Somebody did mouth-to-nose on a cat?" the doctor said. "That's great! Wait till I tell the nurses." Chuckling, he left the room.

"I let go of Pete when Mr. Woolsey shot at me," Alex said. "I wonder why he went back toward the fire instead of running home."

"Maybe he was following you," Mrs. Kendrill said.

"It's a good thing he didn't come home," Mr. Kendrill said. "If he had, Rocky would not have heard you call for help."

"I hope Pete's okay," Alex said. He closed his eyes, trying not to let tears form. If Pete doesn't make it, he thought, it will be my fault. I shouldn't have let him run loose, no matter how much he wanted it. I should have kept him safe.

18

Pete opened his eyes.

"He's awake!" Rocky said. "Pete woke up."

"*Where am I?*" Pete asked. *He lifted his head and looked around.*

"Hi, Petey," Benjie said.

"*Why am I riding in a car?*" Pete said. "*The only time I go in the car is when they take me to the vet. I don't want to go to the vet. I already had my shots this year. Let me out of here!*"

He struggled to get out of Rocky's arms.

"Settle down, Pete," Rocky said. "It's okay."

"He's scared," Benjie said. "He probably knows we're taking him to the vet."

"*I knew it! I knew that's where we're going. I refuse! The vet grabs my tail and sticks a thermometer in me. It's humiliating.*" *Pete dug his front claws into Rocky's jeans and tried to climb down Rocky's leg.*

"Ow!" Rocky said. He held on to Pete's middle, trying not to touch the area on the cat's neck where the fur had been singed. "He's clawing my leg."

"Stop that, Petey," Benjie said.

"Easy for you to say," Pete replied. "You aren't the one heading toward doom."

"I'm going to pull over," Blake said. He stopped on the side of the road, then leaned into the backseat.

Pete growled at him.

"For a cat who just regained consciousness, he is plenty strong," Rocky said.

"I'm a mighty jungle beast!" Pete said.

"Maybe we don't need to take him to the emergency clinic," Blake said. "He doesn't act injured."

"I'm going under the seat," Pete said. "You'll never get me out of there."

"Let's take him home," Benjie said.

"Yes! Take me home!" Pete continued to claw at Rocky's pants.

"I can't hold him much longer," Rocky said.

"We have a cat carrier at home," Benjie said. "When we take him to the vet, he rides in that."

Pete twisted sideways, shoved off with his hind feet, and jumped to the back of Blake's seat. He put his face next to Blake's ear and yowled, "Turn this car around!"

"I'm taking him home," Blake said. "When your parents return, Benjie, they can examine Pete and decide if he needs to be seen by a veterinarian tonight. Clearly, it is not a matter of life and death, and it isn't safe to drive with Pete leaping around the car. He'll do better in his carrier."

"No, I won't!" Pete said. "I detest that carrier. I don't need to see the vet. I'll bite his hand. Except for a headache, I'm strong as a panther."

Blake turned around at the next intersection and headed back to Valley View Estates.

Pete jumped back into Rocky's lap, draped himself across Rocky's knees, and lay still.

Rocky stroked him gently.

As the car started down Valley View Drive, Benjie said, "I thought you were a bad boy, Rocky, but you aren't. You're nice."

"Thanks," Rocky said. "You're nice, too."

"I know who started the fires," Benjie said. "It was the red-white-and-blue monster monkeys. They ride on giant burros and they kidnap children and turn them into garbage cans."

Headlights shone in the car through the side window.

Blake slammed on the brakes, honked the horn, and yanked the steering wheel to the left.

"Watch out!" Rocky yelled.

Pete leaped from Rocky's lap to the floor as a car smashed into the right front side of Blake's car.

Metal scraped against metal; glass tinkled to the pavement. The car shuddered to a stop.

"Are you boys okay?" Blake asked.

"I'm okay," Benjie said.

"So am I," Rocky said.

"*I'm not!*" *Pete yelled.* "*This car is dangerous! I want to go home!*"

"That car ran the stop sign," Blake said. "It never even slowed down." He unbuckled his seat belt. "Hang on to the cat while I get out," he said.

Rocky leaned down, but by then Pete was already under the front seat. That's where he stayed while Blake spoke to the other driver. That's where he stayed while a police officer arrived and got details of the accident, and that's where he stayed after Blake drove back to the Kendrills' house.

Blake, Rocky, and Benjie tried to entice him to come out.

"We're home, Petey," Benjie said. "We'll take you in the house. We'll give you kitty num-num."

"*I don't trust you,*" *Pete said.* "*I want Alex.*"

The phone on the table beside Alex's bed rang.

"Hello?" Mrs. Kendrill said.

After a brief conversation, she hung up. "That was Blake Morris. He had an accident. Somebody drove out of Maple Street onto Valley View Drive without stopping.

Nobody's hurt, but he thought we should know that he and Rocky are at our house with Benjie. Pete woke up before they got to the clinic and caused such a ruckus that they took him home. Now he's under the seat of Blake's car; they can't get him out."

"We need to get home," Mr. Kendrill said.

"I want to go with you," Alex said. "Except for a sore throat and the burns on my arms, I feel fine."

Mr. and Mrs. Kendrill consulted the doctor.

After dressing his burns, the doctor agreed that Alex could leave the hospital.

It was nearly midnight when Alex and his parents turned onto Valley View Drive.

"There's where the accident was," Mr. Kendrill said.

Alex saw broken glass in the street.

"The other driver must have run the stop sign," Mrs. Kendrill said.

"There is no stop sign," Alex said. "It's gone."

Mr. Kendrill stopped the car. He backed up, turning the car so the headlights shone toward where the stop sign should have been. "You're right." The wooden pole lay on the ground; the red stop sign was missing.

"The vandals came back," Mrs. Kendrill said.

"Street signs were bad enough," Mr. Kendrill said, "but when they cut down stop signs, it's dangerous."

Alex said, "Is the stop sign on the other side of the street still there?"

Mr. Kendrill moved the car so they could look. "It's gone, too," he said.

Alex thought about Duke. He had seen Duke and his brother on this street earlier that night. Did they steal the stop signs?

If it was Duke, Alex thought, I should have told Mom and Dad my suspicions when the street signs were cut down instead of waiting until now. An accident could have injured someone, might even have killed Rocky or Benjie. Dad was right; cutting down stop signs was not only wrong, it was dangerous.

"I might know who did it," Alex said.

"Who?" Mrs. Kendrill asked.

Alex told his parents about Duke, and the things he had said. By the time he finished, they were pulling into their own driveway. Even though he had set off to look for Pete that same night, Alex felt as if he had returned from a long journey.

Mr. Morris's car, its front fender and the passenger door crumpled, stood next to the curb.

Benjie ran to greet Alex and his parents. "I was in an accident," he announced.

"Hi, Alex," Rocky said. "Are you okay?"

"My arms look like pink bubble wrap," Alex said, "but I would not be here at all if you hadn't heard me."

"I heard you because I went after your cat," Rocky said.

"Is Pete still in your car?"

"The accident scared him," Mr. Morris said. "We tried to get him out but he won't budge."

"I'll coax him out," Alex said, "but I won't be able to carry him. My arms really hurt where they got burned, and Pete's heavy."

"I'll come with you," Rocky said.

"I'll help," Benjie said.

"You stay here," Mrs. Kendrill said. "Pete is more likely to come to just Alex and Rocky."

Rocky opened the car door.

"Come on, Pete," Alex said. "You're safe now. Come out of there."

Pete's head emerged from under the seat. "Alex!" he said. "I thought you burned up in the fire." He slithered toward Alex.

Rocky reached for him.

"Good boy," Alex said. "Rocky's going to carry you inside for me."

Pete allowed Rocky to scoop him up, then carry him into the house.

"Put him on the clothes dryer so we can get a good look at him," Mrs. Kendrill said. "The light is bright there."

Alex examined the blackened fur on Pete's neck. "His fur got singed but not his skin," he said. He carefully felt all over Pete's body to be sure there were no other injuries. "He has a lump on the back of his head, but I don't think we need to take him to the vet."

"*Quit saying that word,*" Pete said. "*It makes me nervous.*"

Mrs. Kendrill put Pete on the floor. Alex dumped out the contents of Pete's water bowl, then refilled it with fresh water. The cool water soothed Pete's throat. In fact, it soothed his throat so much that he was able to eat half a bowl of crunchies.

The phone rang. After a brief conversation, Mr. Kendrill said, "That was Sergeant Spencer from the police department. They found the missing stop signs in the backyard of two Hilltop boys who have been in trouble before: Lenny and Duke Brainard."

"I told the police about Duke's threats," Rocky said. "I thought he might have started the fires."

"We should have told an adult sooner," Alex said. "We might have prevented the accident."

Mr. Kendrill continued, "The boys claim they went to their uncle's house in Tacoma after school today and got home just before the police arrived."

"That isn't true," Alex said. "I saw them drive away from Maple Street when I was out looking for Pete."

"The police will be interested in that," Mr. Kendrill said. "The car in their driveway was reported stolen earlier today, so the boys were taken to the Juvenile Detention Center."

Relief took the tiredness from Alex. Duke would not be in school on Monday, and without Duke, Henry would be no problem.

"The police also booked Mr. Woolsey on two counts of arson," Mr. Kendrill said, "and they expect to open an investigation into insurance fraud. They found an empty gasoline can in his trunk, and his fingerprints matched those on a can the investigators found earlier today."

"*I found the first can,*" Pete said. "*Get your facts straight.*"

Rocky's mind locked onto just one fact: Mr. Woolsey, not someone from the mob, was the arsonist. The fire that had destroyed their new home had nothing at all to do with Mother's testimony. His eyes met Blake's; Blake smiled at him.

"The police want you to give a statement tomorrow, Alex," Mr. Kendrill said.

"No wonder Mr. Woolsey acted so nervous earlier tonight," Mr. Morris said. "I met him at eight-fifteen and rented a house on Pine Road. We'll still be neighbors."

"That's great," Alex said.

"You are welcome to stay here tonight," Mrs. Kendrill said.

"Can we, Blake?" Rocky asked. "Please?"

"We accept," Mr. Morris said. "The accident knocked out one of my headlights, and I don't like to drive back to the motel that way."

Alex grinned at Rocky. "Since you saved my life," he said, "you can have the bed, and I'll use my sleeping bag on the floor."

"I didn't save your life," Rocky said, "Pete did."

"That's right," Pete said, "and it wasn't easy." In fact, it had been terrifying. Pete decided he would not beg to go outside tomorrow. Even mighty jungle beasts need time to recover from an adventure such as this one.

Half an hour later, Rocky lay in Alex's bed, thinking how glad he was that he and Alex were neighbors. It was good to have a friend again. Even though he still couldn't tell Alex about his past, he now looked forward to the future.

His mother would be home soon, her testimony over. In spite of the danger, Rocky felt proud of what she had done. The witness program had arranged for Blake's former employees to purchase A-One Auto, and Blake would receive payment soon. Meanwhile, he was looking for a different kind of work.

Rocky still missed Nathan, and Rocky the dog, but his loneliness dissolved as he looked forward to spending the weekend with Alex.

Rocky heard a soft rumbling from the floor. At first he

thought Alex was snoring, then he realized it was Pete, purring.

Alex whispered, "Are you still awake?"

"Yes," Rocky replied.

"I was thinking how Pete led you to the fire, and how he stayed there until you heard me yell for help. Most cats would have run away, but Pete didn't. He risked his life to save me."

"Pete's a brave hero," Rocky said.

"Pete deserves kitty num-num for breakfast tomorrow," Pete said.

"I'll give him kitty num-num for breakfast," Alex said.

Pete purred louder. For once, Alex had understood.